Never Say Goodbye

SOFEE SOPHIA

Never Say Goodbye © 2021 by Sofee Sophia

ISBN: 978-1-7372654-1-2

Crystal Hale-Anderson, Editor

Penphoria Publishing Lawrenceville, Georgia 30044

Dedication

I dedicate this book to my Marvelous, James Jamarus.
Thank you, son, for convincing me that I could write it.

Love, Mother

Acknowledgements

Jan Darnell, for her friendship, encouragement, and guidance for the past thirty-plus years.

Lachelle Curry, for the harsh words she delivered when I stumbled and didn't want to continue.

Theresa Kennedy (RIP), who I didn't know personally, but thank dearly for her guidance.

Crystal Hale-Anderson of Penphoria Publishing, for the countless hours of editing my book with me, I appreciate you to the fullest, and may God continue to bless you.

Starbucks, my favorite writing spot in downtown Fort Wayne, Indiana, for never failing to prepare me a fresh, Venti Green Frappe Tea with coconut milk, no whip, and no classic to sip on while creating and laboring in this literary work filled with passion, determination, and faith.

Contents

Testimonies

I met Sophia more than 30 years ago by way of a literacy organization. Back then, she did not realize her power and potential; however, she was fiercely motivated. Reminding me of Dorothy from the Wizard of Oz, who already possessed power within herself to get where she was trying to go, I saw that in Sophia, too. I was like Glinda, the good witch, reminding Sophia, "You have always had the power." After encouraging her, she began to write earnestly, demonstrating a brilliant imagination and empowering the invention of original and entertaining storylines that prove her skill and talent and those that reveal how she puts her soul into all her works. Once Sophia sets her mind to do something, she pursues it until it's finished. She has already written, directed, and acted in several plays and aspires to write more books and movies, which I look forward to reading and watching because I am constantly amazed by her passion for writing. Overall, I find it difficult to put her stories down because they have that non-negotiable and essential quality of making you want to know, "What happens next?!"

~ Jan Darnell ~

Who is Sophia to me? She is nothing less than a spectacular mother who is obedient to the all mighty High, Jesus Christ, and works extremely hard at any and everything she does. Powerful in the sense of her intelligence and creativity when it comes to writing down her bottled-up thoughts, I call her extraordinary for turning her authentic experiences and experiential ideas into masterpieces of art. From the time I was old enough to know who she was up to now, I've been glad, and still am, to be a part of her life. Although there aren't enough words in this universe to describe her and the woman she has become today, in my eyes, she is my...

Spectacular, **O**bedient, **P**owerful, **H**ardworking, **I**ntelligent, **A**mazing, *Sofee Sophia*!

Love, your bonus Daughter

~ April McClain ~

My mother, the definition of a superwoman, came across a lot of kryptonite in life that motivates me to be a better man and husband to this day. When my siblings and I were children, as a single mother, she couldn't say it, but I knew she was afraid, not knowing how she would take care of us or even pay the bills. And I know it hurt her when she saw us disappointed or when we made her cry because we didn't have what we wanted. Nevertheless, she continued to pray for us, provide for us, and watch over us every night we went to sleep.

I remember as a child she wrote a playback in the 80s (one of the best she ever wrote), and someone stole her play, crushing her for years. The devil tried to put her in a mindset of defeat and turmoil. But, OUR HEAVENLY FATHER gave her the spirit of PERSEVERANCE to continue writing, acting, and producing to create a legacy for our family. A legacy to hand down to generations and generations that one day her great, great, great grandkids will see her works and hear about her struggles, shortcomings, and defeats. They, too, will put her with the likes of Martin Luther King, Harriet Tubman, and Madame CJ Walker and deem their grandmother as a pioneer who never allowed hard times and adversity to stop her.

I remember a time when my siblings and I were eating in the kitchen and my mother dancing around to Lauren hill, saying how GOD was going to bless us to be on television one day because of the plays and productions we'd write. The more she talked about it, the more I likened her to a flower growing through a crack of concrete. My mother was tough and resilient, and no one could stop her. To this day, GOD has given her sufficient strength to prevail in the face of adversity. With the mind of a genius, qualities of a PROVERBS 31 WOMAN, and the eyes of a tiger, my mother has everything she needs to crack the code to her definition of success.

The moral of the story is she taught us that no matter how long it takes to accomplish our goals—and it may take years—to keep striving and persevering no matter what because the devil can never stop what GOD has for us.

Love you momma,

~ **Telly** ~

SoSoe, the creator! I love the creative energy she brings when her mind gets to going! She makes anyone feel as if they can do anything! Creative, artistic, intelligent, and ever-evolving into realms, conquering them like a true professional. I will forever be proud of the professional paths that Sophia pursues, and I encourage her to keep evolving, keep pressing, keep pushing, and keep following the voice of God that will lead her to her destiny!

Love,

~ Raven Sykes ~
The best damn daughter-in-law in the whole world!

Ever since I was a young boy, I remember having so much fun while my mom and her fellow castmates practiced on stage. Most of my memories are of those watching my mom's creativity at work. I am proud of everything that she has accomplished, and I can't wait to see what's next for her.

Love you mom,

Your son,
~ James (Marvelous) ~

The words I want to express aloud for my mother's natural-born talent would sound like pure silence because I'm always astounded as her writing is captivating, awe-inspiring, and the kind that arrests your attention. How she has you waiting on the edge of your seat, reaching for breath and receiving it, then slowly exhaling it leaves you speechless, pondering about how and where she came up with her creative, fascinating, and riveting ideas. As she thoroughly expresses her thoughts and experiences on every page, whether authentic and personal, vicarious or relatable, experiential and imaginative, you applaud the writer in your head while thinking, *job well done.*

Sophia, Mother Dearest, *Never Say Goodbye* is your new baby, and I'm happy to call it my new sibling. I'm so excited for you both, and I can't wait to see him grow. I Love you, Mother Dearest, Congratulations!

~ Helen Sykes ~

To my grandmother and one of my mentors and best friends, thank you for teaching me every day that no matter my age, I can do anything I set my mind to do and achieve what I want in life. Thank you for encouraging me and showing me not to be afraid of anyone or anything and strive to be my best self. Thank you for loving and caring for those around you even when you are or feel that you're at your worst. Thank you for all the ways you care for and love me—always.

~ Love, Zarie ~

I met Sofee eleven years ago at a casting call for her movie *21 Days Absent*, a story about her family, to audition for the role cast as her. I didn't get the part. But what I did get was so much more, a friendship and unbreakable bond we developed throughout the years, only to find out that we are distant cousins. At the time, I thought, "NOW WE FAMILY." By working so closely with Sofee, I've witnessed her birth many plays, movies, and short stories, and I would hear her often say, "I can hear the characters talking." So, it was inevitable that she would eventually take one of those characters in her head and write a book all about him.

This book, *Never Say Goodbye*, came from an original script inspired by a little boy named George who would serve as a voice for children who went through traumatic experiences birthed from tragedies they either witnessed or lived through at a young age. Unfortunately, and more often than not, when children's emotions go unchecked, the risk of them going down dark paths becomes greater. Sofee tells a story that perfectly describes how trauma, when unaddressed, can impact children in the worst way. While she dives deep into the life of the main character, George, to depict how trauma groomed him to become a serial killer, she takes readers on a journey of holding space to have compassion for him rather than hating him. To refrain from giving too much of the story away, I encourage you to grab some cookies, a nice cup of tea, a warm, snuggling blanket, get comfy, and prepare for this emotional roller-coaster ride on which *Never Say Goodbye* will take you.

Sofee, I love you and ask that you please continue to give us your passion—writing.

~ Yuzetta Anderson ~
Assistant Director, Associate Producer, Actor

I met SoSo through her niece, Rochelle, at a local gym. I informed Rochelle that I was working on a production and needed help, and she recommended SoSo. We connected and have been sisters ever since. It didn't take long for us to begin working together on the *Dreams* project, where she served as a vibrant acting coach and aided in the production to make it a hit! We found a way to improve our weaknesses together and build on each other's strengths to have a winning chance of presenting an impactful and successful production. She is a creative, gifted, talented, and explosive writer! I can't wait to work together on our next project!

~ Karen Baker ~
Producer, Director

As we bridge 2021, after a trying year for many, we reawaken, in a sense, to a new beginning. Many people kept their sanity by tapping into their imagination and creative genes. I know first-hand, as the owner of *Kustom Kreations Exclusive*, a custom print shop and event planning business based in Indianapolis, Indiana, Sophia took all that energy—good and bad—and poured it all into this suspense/thriller.

I met Ms. Soe at a live stage play where I was an exclusive vendor offering products promoted specifically for the production. When Sophia approached my table to purchase a t-shirt and coffee mug, as we engaged in conversation, I learned that she was a writer, actress, and producer who successfully put on several amazing productions. I wanted in! She was equally amazed by my work and wanted to order products for an up-and-coming stage play she planned to put on later that year. We stayed in touch, and as the time came near, I auditioned and landed a role in her play. But Covid canceled that as well as any form of social life we had. In the midst of it all, Sophia willfully managed to write this incredible book.

This thriller will engage you, draw you in, and compel you to connect with a diverse lineup of characters who represent the lives of people from all walks of life. If you ever get the chance to watch the trailer first, you will become hooked on the story and want to know more! I won't do a spoiler alert before you have a chance to read the book, but I will tell you to find a coffee spot or bookstore where you can get comfortable because you won't be able to put this book down. I guarantee you that you will be unable to predict a single twist you encounter. And when you read the end of the book, you will surely make it a conversation piece.

~ Miaesha Caldwell ~

CHAPTER 1

First Kill

One Friday evening, at the Peoples Bar, George Bojack sat enjoying a beer distributed by his business, the *BoJack Distribution Company*. George was a tall, average-looking man with sandy brown hair and green eyes in his early thirties. Another customer sitting at the bar attempted to engage him in a conversation he was having with the bartender.

"Hey buddy," the man said to George, "Did you hear that?"

"No, I wasn't listening," George replied.

"Well, our bartender here is planning to go deer hunting for the first time," the man said while taking a sip of his drink. "I remember my first kill … Plenty of meat. I took down a big buck."

While peering over at the bartender, the man continued to explain, "A buck's what they call a male deer."

The bartender scowled at him and said, "I am very much aware of that."

Turning back to George, the stranger asked, "Hey, buddy? You ever go hunting?"

Pausing before answering, George replied, "Yes, I have. But my first kill was a female."

George asked the bartender to close his tab. While waiting for his receipt and drinking the last sips of his beer, he began to daydream about that day. He drifted back to the classroom at Wells Heights Elementary School when he was in the fourth grade.

Ms. Hensley was his teacher. George did not appreciate her for failing to utter a word when, as he stood in front of the class presenting his report, the other students teased and laughed at him. He became so angry that he knocked most of the items off her desk onto the floor, bringing her and the other students to a stunned silence. Holding back her anger, she took a deep breath before slowly, in a whisper, counting to three.

"George, please leave," she said calmly, "And go to the principal's office."

He glanced around the classroom and noticed smirks on some students' faces and the looks of disbelief on others. As he turned back to face and address Ms. Hensley, she placed her left hand on her hip, and with her other hand pointed toward the classroom door. She allowed the one word he hated with a passion to spill from her mouth, the one that a few of his classmates constantly used to tease him because they knew how he would react when anyone would say it.

"Goodbye!" she shouted.

George froze. He tried to move his feet but couldn't and looked as if he was in a trance. Ms. Hensley repeated herself. This time with more authority she added his name.

"Goodbye, George!"

Outraged, with his arms at his sides, he balled up his fists and stomped his feet, and proceeded to leave the classroom. Tyrese, George's number one enemy and the class clown, mocked him in a silly voice as he passed his desk.

He whispered, "Goodbye George, goodbye George, goodbye George, goodbye…."

The entire class burst out into laughter as he approached the door. Pausing, he looked back at Ms. Hensley with evil intent. She had now become his number one enemy. Then he left.

After storming out of the classroom, with all of his might, he slammed the door so hard that it bounced back open a few times. Silence fell over the classroom. George stood there, wiping tears from his eyes.

Tyrese then yelled out, "He's crazy! That dude is *crazy!*"

Again, the entire class burst into laughter.

"Settle down so that we can get back to work," Ms. Hensley told them.

She asked if a few students would help pick up the items from the floor and place them back onto her desk. Everyone except Tyrese raised their hands. After choosing which students to assist her, Ms. Hensley instructed everyone else to put away everything on their desks because it was time for the pre-test on words and definitions.

"I hope each of you studied because the scores you receive on the test this Thursday will set the tone for Friday.

Will you have a fun day, or will you have a not-so-fun day?" she asked.

Tyrese whispered to another student that he did not need to study because of his photographic memory. Ms. Hensley heard what he said. Wanting to prove him wrong, she flipped through her spelling book and looked for a word she thought he might not know. She snickered before asking him to stand and spell ichthyology, followed by its definition.

Tyrese stood up and looked perplexed. "Ike the who?"

The students couldn't help themselves and burst into laughter yet again. Threatening to take away their recess, Ms. Hensley told the class to settle down.

Brenda raised her hand and asked, "May I spell it and give you the definition, please?"

"Of course, Brenda, go ahead," replied Ms. Hensley.

After she spelling the word, Brenda told the class, "It means the study of fish."

Tyrese, mischievous as ever, blurted out, "No wonder I couldn't spell it; I'm allergic to fish!"

This time his classmates tried to smother their laughter as Ms. Hensley explained that food allergies are not funny.

"By the way, I'm allergic to fish myself," she said with irritation. "During an allergy attack, if my throat swells up, it can close completely. And if I do not receive medical attention right away, I can die."

The room gasped. Ms. Hensley then pulled out her EpiPen to show the class what it looked like and explained the importance of always having it near her.

George hovered in the hallway the entire time watching his teacher through the cracked door, listening to her every word. He wasn't like other kids.

CHAPTER 2

False Alarm

From a young age, George lived in foster homes, and for the last two months, he had been living with his foster sister, Rachel. She took good care of him and made sure to help him settle into his new way of life.

A few days later, after the incident at school, with much persistence, George convinced Rachel to take him to the pet store to purchase a goldfish. After choosing the perfect fish, they stood in line waiting to buy it.

"This line is moving way too slow and needs to move a bit faster, or we are going to miss the last bus," Rachel said, "and I sure don't have enough money for a taxi."

Another cashier opened up checkout lane number five, and she rushed over to be the first in line. After paying for the fish, she and George rushed out of the store without a single moment to spare. After boarding the bus and paying their fare, George took an open seat near the back and set his goldfish down beside him, and Rachel sat directly behind him. Suddenly, she spotted a spider on the back of his seat, shouting and demanding him to kill it. Turning around, he sat on his knees and briefly held onto the bar that was attached to his seat. Letting go, he smashed the spider with his bare hand and then wiped it off on his pants.

"I'm not afraid you know," he said unemotionally.

"You're not afraid of what?" asked Rachel.

"I'm not afraid to kill."

"I know that already. I've witnessed you kill many spiders."

She pulled the release cord so that they could exit the bus at their intended stop. Getting off first, George ran toward their apartment. But suddenly, he turned around and ran back towards Rachel, yelling to her to stop the bus.

"What did you say?" she yelled back.

"Stop the bus! I left my fish on the bus!" he responded, panicking.

The bus had already pulled off by the time she understood what he was saying.

Later on that night, when George was in his bedroom playing video games on his tablet, Rachel knocked on his door. Her nightly routine was to spend at least ten minutes with him before his bedtime.

"Come in!"

"Dude, did you brush your teeth?"

"Yup."

"Sure, you did," she laughed. "Now, put your tablet away. It's late. Climb on into bed and let me tuck you in."

She pulled the blanket up over his body.

"Listen up, kiddo! How about going back to the pet store and buying another goldfish in a few days?"

George thought about it. "No, thanks. But how about a puppy?"

Rachel gave him a wink, followed by a huge smile. While kissing his forehead she said, "That's not going to happen. But, I do have something I really need to ask you."

"Okay, ask away."

"Would you be okay with me calling you my little brother rather than my foster brother?"

Showing his approval, George jumped up from the bed, embraced Rachel, and gave her the biggest hug ever.

She then grabbed his hand, locked their pinky fingers, and told him, "Our bond is unbreakable, and no one will ever come between us."

George hugged Rachel again before she tucked him back into bed.

On this particular night, he was on a mission. After Rachel left his room, he listened for her bedroom door to shut before getting up again. Once he had the all-clear to move forward with his plan, he retrieved the pair of scissors he hid under his pillow, jumped out of bed, and grabbed the goldfish he hid in one of his high-top sneakers. He didn't like lying to his sister, but he couldn't reveal his motive for purchasing the fish and pretending to leave it on the bus. It was the perfect time for him to prepare and follow through on his revenge against Ms. Hensley.

George laid down a big towel, set the scissors down on it, picked up the bag that housed the fish—watching it swim back and forth—then cut the corner of the plastic bag and let the contents spill onto the towel. He then laid down next to the goldfish and watched it gasp as it struggled to breathe without water. He imitated the fish, gulping for air until it was dead.

George woke up early the following morning and listened for Rachel to take her shower. After the bathroom door closed, he hopped out of bed, tiptoed into her room to use her cell phone, and sent a text message to one of the school administrators to communicate that he had a dentist appointment that morning.

The administrator texted back. "Will George return to school after his dentist appointment? Followed by your answer, please include your assigned authorization code. Thank you for your cooperation."

Only parents or guardians should know their unique codes, but George knew Rachel's because he found it while snooping around in her room one day. He replied to the text with a message and the code as requested.

"Yes, he will return around lunchtime. The code is 2237."

George went back into his room and rehearsed his game plan.

For once, Ms. Hensley's class was calm. Grouping the students into four separate groups, she tasked each of them with working on a different project. Unfortunately for Tyrese, he had to sit at the desk with Ms. Hensley to complete some week-old homework. Eighteen minutes before lunch, the fire alarm sounded.

"Can someone explain why there is a fire drill right before lunch?" Tyrese asked in a demanding tone.

"I'm hungry and ready to eat," he whined.

Ms. Hensley exhaled before answering his question. "It could very well be a real fire."

"Or, maybe someone pulled the fire alarm for no reason," replied Tyrese.

Cutting him off, Ms. Hensley responded, "Tyrese, I'll deal with you later. We don't have time for your shenanigans."

She directed her attention to the entire class and spouted out commands.

"Focus up, class. You all know the drill. Form a single file line, remain quiet when leaving the room, and walk calmly to the nearest exit. Now, let's skedaddle."

Ms. Hensley was the last to leave, shutting the door behind her. About two minutes later, the door slowly opened, and George entered the classroom. After placing his backpack on Ms. Hensley's desk, he took her EpiPen from the top drawer and put it in his pocket. After retrieving her lunch from the bottom drawer, he sat it on the desk and removed the lid. Grabbing a sandwich bag filled with a substance that resembled minced meat from his backpack, George mixed it in with her spaghetti, stirred it up with his pointer finger, and licked off what was left.

The students were still standing outside when the principal announced with his bullhorn three times, "False alarm, false alarm, false alarm."

Tyrese said out loud, "Go ahead, Ms. Hensley. You can say it, I was right."

She ignored him and focused on listening to the principal.

"Attention, all teachers! If your students eat during the first-period lunch, the bell will ring in seven minutes. Please direct them to the cafeteria."

CHAPTER 3

EpiPen

After dropping the students off at the cafeteria, Ms. Hensley walked back to her classroom. Ms. Nichols, another teacher, was waiting for her outside of the classroom door.

She asked, "What was the matter with your problem child the other day?"

"Oh, George, the psycho boy?" Ms. Hensley whispered. "So, the episode unfolded when one of my other students said goodbye to him. He started screaming, jumping up and down, and crying. On three different occasions in the last five weeks, he had a breakdown and threw a tantrum like a toddler. I requested a psych evaluation each time," she explained in a gossiping manner.

Ms. Nichols leaned in and said, "Clearly, they know something we don't, which might be the reason they haven't mandated and ordered an evaluation."

"This time, I requested a room change. Tyrese and George cannot be in the same classroom together. They must separate. And, to be honest, I would rather deal with the class clown over a kid who throws tantrums."

"Please do not send your psycho boy to me," asserted Ms. Nichols.

They both giggled like schoolgirls. Ms. Nichols then told Ms. Hensley her plan to pick up lunch from across the street and asked if she wanted to join.

"No, thank you. I brought my lunch, and everyone knows how much I love cold spaghetti. Besides, I have a few more papers to grade."

"Okay, I'll grab my lunch and join you. Be right back."

Sitting down and then searching for hand sanitizer, Ms. Hensley had no clue her EpiPen was missing. After taking her Tupperware lunch container from the bottom drawer, sanitizing her hands, and removing the lid, she sniffed her food and prepared to eat. Not paying any attention to her senses, she stirred the spaghetti with a fork before consuming her first bite.

After grading her first paper, she took a second bite. Immediately, she noticed hives popping up on her hands, and she frantically began to search for her EpiPen.

"It has to be here."

As hives continued to cover her body, she became more and more anxious. A full-fledged anxiety attack caused her throat to swell shut. Her antidote gone, she gasped for air. While grabbing her constricting throat, she stood up and struggled to get to the hallway. After taking only two steps, she fell to the floor. With all the strength she had left, she tried crawling and yelled for help. Tears fell from her eyes as she remembered Ms. Nichols had shut the door behind her. Seeing from her peripheral vision, she saw George holding her EpiPen. She desperately reached out to him, gesturing to him to give her the pen. Instead of helping his teacher live, he laid down beside her and mocked her by gasping for air just as he did with the fish. His actions scared her to death.

A few minutes later, George walked to the cafeteria and requested his lunch. He sat at a table by himself, waiting to hear the sound of sirens. As the ambulance, fire truck, and a couple of police cars pulled up, every student, except him, got up from their tables and ran to the window.

One student blurted out, "What happened?"

"I don't know, but it must be terrible," another student replied.

George got up from his seat and walked over to the window. He stood directly behind Tyrese and whispered, "Tell no one of what I'm about to say. Never say *goodbye* to me ever again, or you will stop breathing, too."

Trembling, Tyrese was too afraid to respond. After picking up his backpack and quietly leaving the cafeteria, George noticed that Ms. Nichols was crying as she spoke to a police detective.

The bartender interrupted George's thoughts when she gave him his receipt. "Sir, will it be cash or charge?"

"Oh, oh, sorry about that. Charge, ma'am," he responded while handing his credit card to her.

On the following Monday morning, BoJack Beer company managers attended the mandatory weekly meeting. Everyone noticed two unfamiliar faces in the conference room. When George entered, silence fell upon the room.

"Good morning, everyone," he greeted.

"Good morning," everyone replied harmoniously.

George stood behind the podium and called the meeting to order. "This meeting and my message will be short and sweet. The BoJack Beer Company is no longer ranked number two."

One of the male managers interrupted, "I hope we didn't go backwards."

"Short and sweet, because of the consistency and loyalty of our team here at BoJack, when it comes to providing superior customer service and achieving 100% on-time delivery, we now rank number one in the industry. And you'll be glad to know that the *Tasteful Beer Magazine*, a reputable company in the publishing industry that rates companies like ours, wants to give its congratulations and honor our company at its upcoming conference."

All the managers reacted by clapping and whistling.

A female manager asked, "Mr. George, now that we're ranked number one, should we expect to receive a bonus anytime soon?"

"If we stay in this position for at least the next three months, yes," he replied.

Everyone applauded, whistled, and chatted amongst themselves.

"Settle down, everyone, settle down. Given that I'm attending the conference next week, I'll be gone for several days. Now, next on my agenda, I'd like to introduce all of you to our two newest employees. Everyone, say hello to Chase Outright and Pilar K'teace.

The new employees each stood up when George called their names.

"Chase will work in central supplies with you and your team, Clark, and Pilar K'teace will work in the warehouse with Derrick and his team. Let's welcome them with open arms and make them feel at home."

In unison, the managers applauded and gave them a warm welcome. Pilar and Chase waved and thanked everyone.

"The last thing on my agenda is to announce the employee of the month: Catrina Malloy, my administrative secretary."

As soon as George spoke her name, Catrina rushed into the conference room.

"My apologies, Mr. George. I was on the phone with a potential customer," she said hurriedly.

"What about our employee of the month?"

"I don't know, sir. You never got around to telling me who it is so I could put their name on the plaque."

George chuckled. Catrina looked around the conference room, wondering what was up with everyone.

"Catrina?" George spoke quite loudly.

"Yes, Mr. George?"

"You're the employee of the month."

"Me?" Catrina squealed. "Is that why you evaded the subject every time I brought it up?"

"Yes, Catrina."

George looked at his watch and quickly ordered his staff to get back to work. Before they left, he gave them a reminder.

"And everyone knows that when we leave, the company policy mandates that you never say *goodbye* in my presence. We say...?"

In concert, everyone answered, "See you later."

Mumbling to Chase, Pilar said, "That's odd."

All the managers, including Pilar and Chase, left the conference room.

Catrina cleared her throat before she began to advise George.

"Mr. George, your itinerary is complete. Both cities. Would you like car service with a driver or a car rental?"

"In Chicago, I'd prefer car service, but I'd like to have a rental car when I visit my sister in Fort Wayne. Will you arrange both for me?"

"Okay, got it! Your flight leaves Indy Tuesday at 11:00 a.m. What time would you like your driver to arrive at your home?"

"Around 6:00 a.m."

"Okay. As soon as I get back to my desk, I'll email you all the information and add the details to my calendar."

"Thank you, Catrina, you're the best!"

"You're welcome, sir. The pleasure is always mine."

"Oh, I forgot to tell you," George said, turning around. "For lunch, I'll be eating at Auntie Momma's Kitchen."

"And what time is lunch?"

"11:30 a.m."

"Mr. George, what about your 11:30 am meeting with Mr. Harper?"

"Call and cancel it."

"Yes, sir!"

"As for your sister, she has yet to answer or return any of my calls."

"She hasn't answered any of mine either."

CHAPTER 4

Ol' Betsy

George was about to order his lunch at the restaurant when he noticed a woman standing outside the window. She was letting her hair down out of a ponytail and shaking it loose. George realized it was Pilar and thought to himself, *She is gorgeous, and her hair is so full and beautiful.* The waitress approached and asked him if she could take his order. He sprung up and tossed his napkin on the table. By then, Pilar had walked away.

The waitress asked, "Sir, is everything okay?" George stared out the window and replied, "Yes. I will be right back."

When he stepped outside, he looked up and down the sidewalk and didn't see Pilar until she crossed the street. He followed her across the street and discreetly walked into the department store. He lost sight of her and eventually spotted her admiring several outfits designed by Vaness Louez, her favorite fashion designer. From behind a pillar, he hid out and watched her as she modeled several outfits and listened intently to the conversation she was having with the clerk.

He overheard the clerk tell her, "You looked great in all the outfits, but I think the last one is over the top. Honestly, you should buy it."

Pilar looked at the price tag and said, "Two hundred and fifty dollars for two pieces! No way! I can buy groceries and pay my light and gas bills for this amount."

Admiring herself in the mirror, she told the clerk, "Girl, you should know by now that my budget is twenty dollars a week for clothes. Let me take this expensive pantsuit off and head up the street where everything is not so expensive. See you next week, same day, same time."

George watched Pilar walk out of the department store and into the second-hand store where she purchased a pair of jeans and a cute pink tee shirt for seven dollars and fifty cents.

Feeling overwhelmed from a full day, she yawned and said to herself, "It's time for me to go home and soak."

George perked up when she walked out of the store. Unfortunately for him, her timing was perfect. The bus pulled up, and Pilar climbed aboard, riding off into the sunset.

The next day as Pilar was climbing onto the forklift, her co-worker, Chuck, stopped her and yelled in a commanding manner.

"Please do not get on that forklift!"

"Why not?" Pilar asked in a tone of voice that captured the attention of other co-workers standing around.

"I've been standing in this same spot for three days watching you do the same thing repeatedly," Chuck said, looking embarrassed. "It's called orientation, and I think you are a little too delicate to handle Ol' Betsy."

As he climbed onto the forklift, with a gentle push, Pilar politely shoved him off. She climbed back on and showed

Chuck and her co-workers that she might be delicate in appearance, but she could do her job better than they could.

After handling the forklift like a pro, she climbed off and told Chuck, "Don't call her Ol' Betsy anymore; call her Sasha from now on."

As her co-workers cheered her on, she walked away with confidence and with a smirk on her face. Chuck had no choice but to respect her.

Meanwhile, Mr. Bojack was sitting at his desk, searching for Pilar in the employee profiles. He found her background information and a photo and stared into her eyes for a moment before kissing his fingers and placing a kiss gently on her computer-screen lips.

He said to himself, "I'm falling in love with you, Pilar."

As the day went by, Pilar felt she was now a part of the crew, carrying her weight and getting the job done. When the workday was over, she went into the ladies' bathroom to freshen up. She washed her face before putting on a light touch of makeup and letting her hair down. When she came out of the bathroom, she thought it was peculiar to see several of her male co-workers, including Chuck and one female co-worker, gathered outside the bathroom door. She pretended not to notice them and walked ahead. Unexpectedly, one of the guys approached her.

Chuck interrupted her and asked, "Excuse me, Pilar, can I offer you a ride home?"

"No, thank you," she replied. "I'm not too delicate to catch the bus."

Another co-worker, Sharon, asked if she could give Pilar a ride home, too.

Pilar grinned. "Sure, why not?"

Her male co-workers' reactions were priceless. But what they didn't know was Sharon and Pilar were friends who met while attending the same school a few years back.

A breaking news alert popped up on George's computer screen. He pulled up the website and listened intently to the newscaster.

"This morning, a young lady was jogging in the park when she spotted a delivery truck that belonged to her employer, *Coach Carrier*. She approached the truck to say good morning to the driver when she found her co-worker slumped over the steering wheel, dead. The coroner deemed his death a homicide because his skull was cracked open with a metal object."

George's facial expression went dark as he drifted off into his thoughts and began to reminisce about the previous evening when he pulled into his driveway.

Before getting out of the car, he grabbed his laptop and doggie bag from *Auntie Mama's Kitchen*. George was letting himself into the house when a *Coach Carrier* truck pulled up. Not pleased with the conversation he had with his supervisor, which left him somewhat perturbed, the driver, Tim, hung up the phone. Looking for George's packages, he aggressively began to toss them around the truck. Tim rang the doorbell, and George stepped out onto his porch.

"I have a package for Mr. George Bojack."

"That would be me," George replied.

"Please sign here by the X, sir."

After George signed his name, Tim handed him a small package.

"Thanks and have a good evening," George replied.

Still steaming from the conversation with his supervisor, Tim said, "Whatever, man. Goodbye."

Giving Tim a chance to redeem himself, George hesitated. He then asked Tim to read the plaque that hung on his front door:

NEVER SAY GOODBYE.
SAY SEE YOU LATER!

"Yeah, whatever, man," Tim sighed, "Goodbye!"

When Tim was about to pull off in his truck, George walked up and tapped on the passenger side window. Tim rolled down the window and looked at George incredulously.

"What is your problem?"

George pointed a silver 22 at him and said, "Unlock the door!"

"Sir, why are you doing this? Here, take my wallet!"

George hissed at him. "Now, that's two insults you made towards me in less than five minutes." George climbed into the truck and said, "Now drive until I tell you to stop."

A knock at his office door brought him out of his trance. "Come in," George said.

Catrina entered, carrying a cup of coffee.

"Ms. Catrina, must I remind you that it is not in your job description to bring me coffee every morning."

"I know Mr. George, but I don't mind. I also don't mind watering these plants you claim to love so much. I just know how forgetful you can be, so someone needs to help you keep them alive."

"Alright, have at it then! But, Catrina, I was reading over our new employee profiles and saw that Pilar is in college studying business. Do you know of any reason why she did not apply for an administrative position here?"

"I asked her the same thing. She said she needed a job fast, and the only position posted on the hiring board at her school was in the warehouse department. So, she took a chance and figured she would work her way up to administration. She has a 3.8 GPA and she wants to launch her very own wine distribution company one day," Catrina explained.

George spoke under his breath, "Intelligence combined with beauty."

"Did you say something, sir?"

"Oh, no, Catrina, I was just thinking out loud."

CHAPTER 5

*Good Morning,
My Love*

George was asleep dreaming about riding on a carousel with Pilar, watching her enjoy eating a vanilla ice cream cone. At the moment she offered him a taste, his alarm clock sounded off, flashing, 5:00 a.m. He hit the snooze button, hoping to fall back asleep and pick up where he left off in his dream. Before he knew it, the alarm sounded off again. He finally decided to get up to shower and shave. After making a cup of coffee and taking a few sips, the doorbell rang. His driver arrived to transport him to the airport.

"Good morning, Devin."

"Good morning, Mr. G," greeted Devin while opening the back passenger door for his boss to get into the car and before loading his luggage into the trunk.

On their way to the airport, George asked, "Devin, would you like to stop by *Auntie Mama's Kitchen* for breakfast before dropping me off at the airport?"

"Sure, sir," replied Devin.

While Devin drove, George pulled a picture up on his laptop. Winking, he whispered, "Good morning, my love."

Devin glanced in the rearview mirror and asked, "You say something, sir?"

"No," George said in a dry tone.

At the restaurant, the waitress asked if she could take their order.

"Nothing for me except a cup of coffee," answered George.

"How about your breakfast special and orange juice?" replied Devin.

After repeating the order, the waitress took their menus and walked off.

Leaning across the table, George said, "Devin?"

"Yes, sir?"

"I need you to take care of some business for me while I'm away."

The waitress returned with their drinks.

Devin asked, "Who is she, sir?"

Taking a few sips first before responding, George asked, "How did you know?"

"You only offer me breakfast when you want to discuss a female you're interested in. What's her name?"

Staring out the window, visualizing Pilar taking her hair down, George seductively said her name, "Ms. Pilar Kteace," I want her … I desire her.

"Are you talking about that sexy ass redhead who works in the warehouse?"

George did not appreciate Devin's response and adamantly replied, "No, not the sexy ass redhead! PILAR!"

Realizing how angry he made his boss, Devin apologized immediately.

"I'm sorry, you're correct, sir. Her name is Pilar," replied Devin, hiding his smile.

"You know almost every man in the warehouse and a few of the women are hounding after her, right?"

George gave Devin a blank stare.

"Minus me, of course, sir."

"Of course," George mumbled.

The waitress returned and placed Devin's food in front of him. He stuffed the first bite in his mouth. George gave him a blank stare.

"Sir, would you like a bite?"

Sliding an envelope across the table to Devin, he said, "No, but what I would like for you to do is...," and then he paused.

In the envelope was $1,000 and a platinum watch.

"What is this for, Mr. G?"

"I'll explain on the way to the airport. Go ahead and enjoy your breakfast."

After taking the luggage out of the trunk, Devin said, "Mr. G., I have a question for you."

"I'm listening."

"Whatever happened to the two women you had me intercept for you?"

George shrugged nonchalantly. "Samantha told me that I didn't give her enough attention, so she said, *see you later.* Believe it or not, I did see her a few weeks later at the grocery store. As for Becky, she told me *goodbye.* I haven't seen her since and could care less if I see her again."

Reflecting for a brief moment, he said to himself, "If only she had said *see you later,*" while shaking his head as he picked up his luggage and disappeared into the crowd.

Back at the warehouse, at the end of her shift, Pilar committed to her after-work routine. After clocking out, she went into the women's bathroom, washed up, changed her clothes, and applied a small amount of makeup. Thinking everyone had left for the day, she walked out of the bathroom, and there stood her co-workers.

Chuck walked up and handed her a bouquet of roses and a box of chocolates. "We all pitched in."

Laughably, Pilar asked, "You all pitched in to buy me flowers and sweets?"

"We sure did," Chuck said, "and we were wondering if you'd like to go on a date with one of us."

"No way," she said while looking around at her options.

Her laughter echoed as she walked out of the building.

CHAPTER 6

Catch A Ride

While walking toward the company's parking lot entrance, Pilar saw a homeless man standing nearby with a shopping cart filled with everything he owned. She picked a rose from the bouquet Chuck and her co-workers gave to her and handed it to the man.

"What is the special occasion, ma'am?" asked the homeless man.

Pilar then offered him a piece of candy. "How about it's just a wonderful day?" she replied.

The man raised the candy in the air, grinned, and exclaimed, "I'll chew to that!"

After taking the last bite of the candy, he noticed his girlfriend coming towards them, pushing her shopping cart.

"Ma'am, can I have another piece of candy for my lady?" he asked while pointing towards her, "and, can I give her the rose you gave me?"

Pilar smiled. "I don't mind it all. Here, give her the whole bouquet of roses and the box of candy."

His eyes welled up with tears. "I haven't been able to give my lady candy, flowers, or anything nice for a long, long time."

After chit-chatting with the homeless man, Pilar headed to the department store. She modeled some of the new inventory and decided to go to the thrift store to purchase a few pieces of beautiful jewelry. As the cashier handed Pilar her change and receipt, she noticed Devin standing in the back of the store trying to capture her attention, waving and pointing at Pilar.

The cashier said, "Oh yeah, her."

Pilar turned and looked behind her. Devin ducked down behind the rack of coats so that she wouldn't see him.

"I have a package for you," the cashier said.

Pilar looked confused. "For me?" She glanced around the store again. "From whom?"

"Hold on, it will take only a moment for me to go and grab it," the cashier replied.

Devin tried to sneak out of the thrift store quietly, only to remember the cowbell hanging on the door, which rang when someone opened it. Pilar looked to see who was there but saw no one coming or going. The cashier returned carrying five different outfits and handed them over to Pilar.

"Here you go! Aren't they beautiful?"

Pilar noticed immediately that they were the outfits she had tried on at the department store, not even an hour ago. She froze and couldn't utter a single word.

"Are you okay?" asked the cashier.

Tossing the clothes onto the counter and stepping back, she raised her voice and asked authoritatively, "WHERE DID THEY COME FROM, AND WHO BROUGHT THEM HERE?"

Scanning the store, the cashier responded, "Um, I don't know his name, but this guy came into the store earlier and asked me to give them to you."

Pilar snapped back. "Someone has been following me, and that is not cool. Not cool at all!"

Aggressively, she prepared for a battle, put her hair in a ponytail, and ran out of the thrift store, leaving the clothes behind. Moving so fast while exiting the door, she bumped into an intoxicated man and dropped the bag of jewelry she purchased.

"Whoa, baby!" said the drunk. "Can we at least introduce ourselves first?" They call me *Dude*, and your name is?" Pilar ignored the man and went to pick up her bag. Dude picked it up before she had a chance to and refused to give it to her.

Pilar yelled, "Hey, that belongs to me!"

"Maybe, maybe not. What do I get for returning it?" he replied while reaching out and grabbing Pilar's wrist.

You could almost see the steam coming from her ears.

Great, she thought, *first the clothes situation and now a foolish drunk named Dude.*

"Let me go before I hurt you!"

Devin walked up at that moment, stood next to Pilar, and pointed a pistol at the drunk. Both Dude and Pilar put their hands up in the air.

"Put your hands down, Pilar," instructed Devin.

She put her hands down and realized he said her name. She pulled his arm down, lowering his gun, and stood between him and the drunken man. Dude instantly took off running.

Devin yelled after him. "Drop that bag, you bum!"

The drunk dropped the bag and continued to run until he was out of sight.

"How do you know my name?" asked Pilar in a demanding manner.

"Huh? I don't know your name."

"Yes, you do, you said my name." Playing dumb, Devin said, "I did?"

"Yes! You said, 'Put your hands down, Pilar.'"

"I said that?"

"You know you did. Why are you stalking me?"

"Now, hold on here. I am not stalking you!" While pulling out his work badge to prove it, Devin explained, "I work for the beer company. I was headed into the thrift store when I saw you might have been in danger."

Grabbing his badge, Pilar asked, "Which department do you work in?"

"I'm Mr. G's driver. Come to think of it; I know exactly how I know your name. He introduced you as one of the new employees at the last company meeting,"

"Uh, I don't recall you being at the meeting."

The city bus rode by, and Pilar took off running after it. The bus driver noticed her out of his rearview mirror and stopped immediately. Quickly realizing that she had left her bags behind, she gestured for the bus driver to wait. Unfortunately, he pulled off as soon as she turned around to go back to collect her things.

"NO, WAIT, WAIT!" she yelled as the bus sped away. "Shoot, I'm sure that was the last bus for today."

Devin walked over to his car and opened the door, offering Pilar a ride home.

Placing her hands on her hip, she stared at him. Talking to herself, she said, "I have two options. Catch a ride that will cost me my last twenty bucks, or I can jog fifteen blocks ... The latter wins."

She then sat down on the curb to change her shoes.

Staring at her in disbelief, Devin asked, "So, you're really going to run all the way home?"

Standing up and stretching, she replied, "Nope! I'm going to jog," while grabbing her book bag and taking off for home.

CHAPTER 7

You Digging On Devin

On the bus ride to work the following day, Pilar was frustrated with herself because of the lingering thoughts in her head about Devin. She wasn't thinking he could be a stalker who loves to harm women but imagined more about his plump lips and how they would feel connected to hers if they locked lips. And, she couldn't help but recall the muscular physique hidden under his tight-fitting tee shirt and straight-leg jeans and how she would love to jump on his back and have him take her for a horseback ride. She was so deep in her thoughts to the point she would have passed her job and arrived late to work if one of the other passengers hadn't pulled the cord for the driver to stop. As she stepped off the bus, she reminded herself that many men approach her almost daily.

She asked herself, "Why am I focusing on Devin? I don't even know him to lie like that."

While clocking in, she noticed a note with her name on it taped to the time clock, instructing her to go to the administration office. When she walked in, Chase, the other new employee, was sitting in the lobby. They happened to greet each other as Catrina exited out of the workroom carrying a couple of manila folders.

"Good morning, Pilar and Chase," greeted Catrina.

She handed them each a folder with their respective names on it.

"I need a signature from both of you so that I can complete your new employee files. Chase, I believe you only have one sheet to sign. You can go when you are complete," she instructed.

After signing the document, Chase laid the folder on the desk and told the ladies he would see them later.

Pilar was about to stand up when she heard Devin's voice.

"Good morning, Catrina," while waving as he passed by the office.

Catrina noticed when Pilar took a gulp of air and held her breath.

"Morning, Devin," Catrina replied while waving him off at the same time.

When he was out of sight, she rushed over to Pilar and sat down beside her. "My goodness, girl. You can breathe now."

Pilar exhaled and said, "I'm so embarrassed."

Sitting back in her seat with a surprised look on her face, Catrina asked, "You diggin' on Devin aren't you?"

Pilar thought to herself, *Oh my god, what if he's her man? I'm going to get fired. I better keep my mouth closed.*

She looked away as Catrina put her arm around her shoulders and whispered, "Your secret will be safe with me, I promise. I won't utter a word to my brother."

Relief rushed through Pilar's body as she shouted, "*Brother?* I mean," she asked, composing herself, "Devin is your brother?"

"Yes, he is my baby brother."

Pilar couldn't help herself and blurted out, "Any chance he's into stalking women?"

Catrina frowned and looked worried. "Pilar, what are you asking me, and what makes you think that about my brother?"

Pilar hesitated and then decided not to give Catrina a response. "I need to get back to work."

"Okay, but I would like to speak on Devin's behalf," asserted Catrina. "He is not a stalker and wouldn't harm a fly. He's a kind-hearted gentleman who is very single."

Pilar experienced another surge of relief. While exiting the office, Catrina assured her. "Pilar, girl, your secret is safe with me."

At lunchtime, Pilar decided not to eat in the cafeteria because she didn't want to be bothered and followed around by her male co-workers. It was like playing musical chairs. If she paused in front of a table, they'd all rush and take a seat, leaving one standing. To avoid the drama, she sat on Sasha, the forklift, to eat her lunch. And not to her surprise, the boys decided to eat their lunch in the warehouse, too.

A few minutes later, Devin entered the warehouse and walked past the guys. He got their attention when he headed straight towards Pilar.

"Man, look. Why is that chump talking to my girl?"

"Man, you got it twisted; she's going to be my girl!"

Devin called Pilar twice, but she didn't hear him because she had her earbuds listening to music. As he walked in her direction, one of the other co-workers pushed Johnnie to confront him. When Johnnie walked up to Devin, he fist-bumped him.

"What's up, man."

"You got it, Johnnie," replied Devin.

Johnnie pointed at Pilar. "No, I don't have it yet, but I'm working on it, and I'm serious about mine."

"Wait a minute, which is it? Are you working on making her yours, or is she already yours?"

Pilar happened to look back when Johnnie stepped up to Devin's chest and bumped him for his smart remark. With a blast of energy, she called out his name.

"Devin!"

He turned his back to Johnnie and ignored him.

"Hey, Pilar! Actually, I was heading over here to ask you to go to lunch with me. What do you say?"

Pilar felt slightly disappointed. "I ate my lunch already. Besides, I only have...," looking at her cell phone, "seven minutes left before I have to clock in and get back to work."

After stepping down from the forklift, she walked over to Devin and hugged him, trusting herself to let him go.

Johnnie grunted. "You never gave me a hug."

The coworkers sitting behind him took turns shouting out, "Me, either!"

She shook her head in disbelief and sighed.

"Forget them," Devin said, "How about dinner?"

"Sure," shrugged Pilar, "Put my number in your phone."

Patting his pockets, he said, "I'll be right back. I think I left my phone in the car."

She knew this was an opportune time for her to touch him again, so when he turned around to leave, she grabbed his hand and blushed before pulling a pen out of her pocket. While writing her number on the palm of his hand, she said, "Call me after work, and I'll let you know where to pick me up."

Intentionally torturing his co-workers, Devin walked out of the warehouse with a Cheshire-cat grin on his face.

Arriving fifteen minutes early and parking where Pilar told him to, Devin picked Pilar up at the Wristpus Community College at 8:30 p.m. He stood near the back passenger door and then opened it when he saw her exit the school.

When Pilar laid her eyes on him, she whispered to herself, "I choose you, my sexy man."

Interrupting her reverie, Devin called her name. "Pilar!"

The closer she got to the car, she could feel her entire body warming up and wondered if he could feel her energy. She ignored his chivalry, opened the front passenger door, and climbed in. Shrugging his shoulders, he shut the back passenger door and walked to the driver's side to get in.

"So, where to?" asked Devin.

"Home," she replied while looking out the window.

"Home? What happened to dinner?"

"I apologize, Devin, but as my professor was dismissing class, he assigned a pop-up quiz at the last minute. Unfortunately, the assignment is due by 11:00 p.m. tonight. If I want to maintain my 3.8 average, I've got to get on it ASAP. Where is your phone?"

Devin hesitated.

"I don't want to look through it," she assured him, "I just want to put my address in your GPS. I won't be paying attention to the road; I'll be too focused on my assignment."

"Oh," Devin replied while handing over his phone.

As he pulled up in front of her apartment, Pilar said, "Thank you for understanding."

"You're welcome," nodded Devin.

"How about dinner tomorrow night?"

"Unfortunately, I am volunteering at the *Darnell Senior Living Facility* tomorrow. Speaking of which, maybe you can meet me there at 7:00 p.m.?"

"I don't know. I'll have to think about that."

Giggling, she got out of the car. "I'll see you tomorrow."

Before entering her apartment, she thought about blowing him a kiss and if he would blow one back. After mustering up enough nerve, she closed her eyes, whipped herself around, and released a kiss. Slowly opening her eyes, she realized Devin had already left.

"Wait a minute, now. His sister told me he was a gentleman. He didn't even bother to make sure I made it into the house safely. Got me out here wasting kisses," she complained.

Grudgingly, she unlocked her apartment door and slammed it behind her.

CHAPTER 8

Caught Off Guard

Lying on a king-sized bed in his hotel suite, George gazed at Pilar's picture on his laptop while sipping on a nightcap. The trophy he received at the *Tasteful Beer Conference* that evening sat on the nightstand next to him. He decided to check in with Devin to determine if things were going in his favor.

Catching him off guard, Devin saw Mr. G calling his phone and was confident he knew why. To avoid engaging in a discussion about Pilar, his boss' dream girl, while sitting in front of her apartment, he sped off.

"Hello, Mr. G."

"Devin, how are things going?"

Lying, he replied, "Things seem to be going okay."

"Is Pilar interested in me?"

"Actually, sir, she is an incredibly busy young lady. She goes to school, and she volunteers at a senior living facility."

George swung his legs off the bed and sat on the edge. "Devin?"

"Yes, sir?"

Reaching deep within, he belted out in his most demanding voice, "MAKE IT HAPPEN!" and abruptly disconnected the call.

Realizing that he had taken his eyes off Pilar's picture long enough, he carried his laptop with him to the minibar to pour himself another drink. While gazing and admiring her all over again, he heard someone knocking at the door. He looked through the peephole and noticed it was Larry, another business owner he met at the conference.

"Say, George, why don't you come downstairs and shoot a few rounds of pool with me?"

"No thanks, man," George replied, "I'm busy."

"What's her name? Ms. Laptop?" asked Larry.

"Noooo, it's Pilar," he said irritably.

Larry attempted to push past George to enter his suite to get a good look at Pilar, but George shoved him back into the hallway and shut the door in his face. After grabbing his drink, he climbed back into the bed and propped his laptop on his chest.

Completely smitten with Pilar, George became easily distracted while on his business trip. He quickly realized the importance of networking and being present in an environment with other industry movers and shakers. While pouting and grunting, he delicately placed the laptop on the bed to avoid slamming Pilar down. After shifting his disgruntled attitude, he got out of the bed to refresh himself before heading downstairs to join the other CEOs and executives and play nice.

Before leaving the room, he turned back to the laptop and said to Pilar, "My beautiful, sweet darling, I'm sorry I have to go, but I'll be back soon," giving her a virtual kiss through the laptop.

When he sat down at the bar, Larry ordered him a drink. While waiting, he drifted off into a fantasy about Pilar.

George could see her walk past him wearing nothing but a towel. He sat up quickly and asked, "What's on your mind?"

Responded seductively, Pilar said, "You and your thoughts about my new body art."

"Why would you destroy your beautiful body with an awful tattoo?" he asked.

Giggling, she dropped the towel to reveal her ink. "Read it ... out loud," she said.

"Okay," he replied, "This belongs to George Bojack." While in aww, he asked, "Oh, is that right?" He then said, "By the way, I love the direction the arrow is pointing."

George grabbed Pilar by the hips, pulled her in close, and kissed her all over before following the arrow. As he explored her most sensitive areas, every time he came up to breathe, he asked, "Will ... you ... marry ... me?"

Panting, she replied, "Only if you promise never to say goodbye."

He stopped and sat next to her, looking into her eyes, connecting to her soul. "My heart belongs to you," he pledged. "Your essence never leaves me. I would never say those words to you."

Whispering, Pilar gave him her answer. "Yes, I'll marry you."

Larry tapped George on his shoulder, interrupting his fantasy. It aggravated him to be sitting at the bar waiting for a pool table to avail. He wanted to get it over with. Sighing and whispering to himself, he said, "I should have stayed upstairs."

"No, man, I heard you. What we should do is a toast to a wonderful conference and our last night in Chicago." Larry took a few swigs of his beer.

"I'd rather toast to my fiancé," murmured George.

Larry abruptly stopped drinking and asked, "Fiancé? Fiancé? Bartender!"

The bartender responded. "Another round of drinks for you fellows?"

"Sure, and not only just for us, but everyone at the bar," Larry shouted.

The bartender leaned over and asked quietly, "You sure, sir?"

"Yes, I'm sure. Give them another round of whatever they're drinking." Larry laid three one-hundred-dollar bills on the bar.

"What's left goes into your pocket."

"Wow, thanks!" exclaimed the bartender. "What's the occasion?"

"Well, my friend, George here, proposed to his girlfriend! ... When? Hell, I don't know, but she said yes! So, to celebrate, everyone sitting at this freaking bar is getting drinks on me!"

Cheering and clapping, everyone congratulated George, which embarrassed him and annoyed him more than anything else at that moment.

"Thank you, thank you," George said while lowering his voice to confront Larry.

"Man, what was that all about? Did you really have to share my personal business?"

"Yes, buddy, yes. This is great news!"

After the bartender poured all the drinks, Larry stood up and asked everyone to raise their glasses to toast George on his engagement. He then leaned over and asked George, "And, what's her name again?"

"It's Pilar."

"Huh?"

"Her name is Pilar," George grumbled.

"To George and Pilar, an authentic love...!" Larry exclaimed and raised his glass.

Everyone repeated after him, cheered some more, and threw back their drinks. When he sat back down, he looked at George in all seriousness.

"So, when is the wedding?"

"She has yet to pick a date. But, I want us to tie the knot on her birthday, next fall in October," George replied.

CHAPTER 9

Rock It Out Bingo

Devin knew how badly his boss wanted Pilar and was counting on him to make it happen. The next day he went to the *Darnell Senior Living Facility* at 7:00 pm to make some progress despite his lack of confidence and the notion that Pilar might be interested in George.

When he drove up to park his car, Angel, Pilar's friend, pulled up behind him. She and Pilar both came to volunteer. Pilar got out of the car, rushed over to him, and gave him an enthusiastic hug. "I can't believe you came," she said excitedly.

"Oh, no! We can't do this," Devin said abruptly as he gently pushed Pilar off him.

Glaring at him with a confused look on her face, she said, "Oh, okay."

Devin backed away and thought to himself, *Damn, she felt good! Woah, snap out of it, Devin. If I want to keep my job, I have to stay focused and handle my business.*

To cut the awkwardness in the air, he changed the subject. "I decided to come because I thought it might be fun."

"It is fun," Angel said, getting out of the car to join them. "These seniors are hilarious!"

She extended her hand and introduced herself. "Hello, my name is Angel."

"Hey, I'm Devin. It's nice to meet you."

While shaking his hand, Angel did not want to let go. When he tried to pull away, she pulled him in closer. She was at least two feet shorter than him and ended up against his chest. If she had been any taller, they would have been lip to lip.

"Mmmm," she hummed. "Boy, do you smell nice!"

Prying them apart, Pilar asked, "Angel? Really?"

Batting her eyes, Angel apologized to Devin.

Pilar giggled. "Girl, is there something in your eyes?"

Angel shrugged her shoulders and shook her head no.

Replying territorially, Pilar said, "Girl, you need to stop because I already have my eyes on that fine ass man. Come on, so we can play bingo with these old folks."

Angel walked ahead of Pilar and Devin.

"Devin, I wasn't expecting her to be so dramatic."

"No harm done! I'm good."

Thinking it would throw Pilar off, he added, "Besides, shorty's kinda' cute."

After they entered the building, Devin walked off to create distance between them. Standing there with her arms cross, Pilar bit her bottom lip and wondered why this man was playing so hard to get.

In the activities room, another volunteer, Robin, called off the bingo numbers in a monotonous voice, "I...   17."

"We need a new bingo caller!" Mr. Johnson yelled out. While pointing at Ms. Daisy, he complained, "She's putting people to sleep again."

The other seniors burst out laughing.

Raising her head, Daisy replied, "I ain't asleep, but I'm about to go to sleep," and put her head back down on the table.

Devin went and stood next to Pilar. "I hate to say it, but you know they're right. Her voice is like a sleeping pill." Suggestively, he asked, "Why doesn't she jazz it up a bit?"

"She's afraid that if she does, she might cause one of them to have a heart attack."

"B.........3."

Mr. Johnson and two other seniors yelled out at the same time, "Bingo!"

Robin stood up. "Pilar, while you guys check their cards for bingo, I'm going to head to the ladies' room. I'll be right back."

As soon as she left the room, Mr. Johnson yelled out again, "Somebody, please lock the door behind her."

Angel jumped right on it and granted Mr. Johnson's request. She didn't think twice about locking Robin out. She remarked, "Oops, somebody locked the door."

Mr. Johnson pointed at Devin. "Now, young man, you look to be up to the job. Why don't you go up there and show us what you're working with?"

"Noooo, siree, you don't want me up there," replied Devin. "I will turn this place out."

Lifting her head from the table, Daisy said, "Turn it out, son. Turn. It. Out."

Laughter roared across the room.

After checking the previous bingo winners' cards, Devin connected his phone to the house speakers.

"Attention, ladies and gentlemen! We are about to play some *Rock It Out* bingo. You better keep up because it's gonna be a fast game," he explained.

Pilar looked at Devin. Assuming he knew what she would say, he said, "Calm down, sis," holding one kind hand up. "I got this."

Pilar thought to herself, *No, he didn't just call me sis?*

"As I was saying," Devin continued, "this game is fast. And, as soon as we get a bingo, I'm going to turn up the music. And when I do, I want you guys to show me your best dance moves. Angel? You ready?"

Angel answered in a seductive voice, "Ready, willing, and able."

Mr. Johnson looked at her and asked everybody, "Do y'all see the heat-generating around that girl?"

Laughter roared across the room again, and Pilar gave Devin the meanest look she could muster.

He shrugged his shoulders and called his first bingo number, "O-75."

As he continued to call out the numbers as quickly as he could, it surprised Pilar to see the seniors keeping up. The game lasted only two minutes when someone called bingo.

Devin asked Angel to call the numbers back to him quickly. "B-5, O-16, O-23, G-47, and G-55!"

"Ladies and gentlemen, we have ourselves a bingo winner!" he cheered, "Give that lady a Mister Goodbar!"

He then turned on the music, and whether they were sitting or standing, everyone started dancing.

Ms. Daisy blurted out, "Y'all, look at me! Check out my dance moves. This game is fun!"

There was a loud knock on the door. Everyone paused, and silence fell over the room.

While yanking on the door and being unable to open it, Robin shouted, "Is something wrong with the door? Why can't I open it? Is it jammed?"

Mr. Johnson yelled back, "No, it's not jammed; it's locked. Y'all, leave her behind out there. She gon' come back in here and ruin our fun. Boy, crank that music back up. This ain't no damn sleepover; it's a dance party."

Devin laughed out loud and did exactly what Mr. Johnson said. Everyone continued to get their groove on.

When Robin saw a facility employee walking by, she asked her to unlock the door to the activities room. When the employee let her in, she couldn't believe her eyes. The seniors appeared to be having no cares or worries and were enjoying themselves to the fullest. She thought to herself, "This is a heart attack waiting to happen."

No one noticed her standing there until she started waving her hands and yelling, "What in the world is going on in here?"

Robin gestured to Devin to turn down the music.

After realizing Robin was back in the room, she killed their vibe. The residents then gathered their belongings and prepared to leave because they knew the party was about to end.

"Wait!" she cried. "Where are you all going? We still have an hour to play bingo and serve cake and ice cream!"

Mr. Johnson stopped in his tracks. "Lady, listen here. Don't nobody want your cake or your ice cream! The cake is probably leaning, and the ice cream is damn sure melted. And, we don't want your sorry ass bingo game either."

The other seniors nodded their heads in agreement.

Ms. Daisy said, "We heard you were going to be ill next week, so he'll back to play bingo with us," while looking over at Devin.

Robin brushed past Devin and shouted, "I don't like you!" and stormed off.

"Pilar? Are we going to get fired?" Angel asked worriedly.

"How does a volunteer get fired?" Pilar asked snarkily.

Devin couldn't help but laugh. At this point, everyone left the room because the party was definitely over.

After getting into her car, Angel honked her horn and said, "Thanks for coming, Devin!"

He waved back and replied, "The pleasure was all mine. I had a great time after all."

Whispering under her breath, Pilar said, "I've had enough of her." Pilar then said out loud, "You were amazing! The seniors fell in love with you. We all did!"

Although indirectly, she couldn't help but express her feelings.

Devin ignored Pilar's comment about love and asked her, "So, what do you think about Mr. G?"

Taken aback, she looked at him with disgust written all over her face.

"Seriously, why are you asking me about him right now?" She changed the subject. "By the way, do you mind dropping me off at home tonight?"

Devin agreed and proceeded to get into the car. Pilar walked around to the passenger side and stood there.

"What are you doing? Are you going to get in?"

"Sure, after you come and open my door for me. That's what a gentleman would do anyway."

"Well, the last time I attempted to open the door for you, you rudely ignored my kind gesture."

She continued to stand there with her arms crossed.

Devin got back out of the car and walked to the other side to let her in. While opening the passenger door, Pilar ran her hand down the middle of his back and then caressed his muscles. Before he could react to her being touchy-feely with him, she received a text message alert.

"Oh My Goodness! Not right now, professor," she groaned. Turning to Devin, "Unfortunately, I have another pop-up quiz with only two hours to turn it in."

CHAPTER 10

Platinum Visa Card

A ngel called Pilar to ask if she had received the
professor's text message.

"Yesssssss, I received it, too," she whined.

"Well, would you like to figure this out together?"

"Sure. Devin, I'm going to ride with Angel after all so
that we can knock this thing out."

She got out of the car, stuck her head in through the
window, and said, "Thanks again for coming."

"The pleasure was all mine!" he responded. "Say, how
about I bring that burger to you for lunch tomorrow?"

"I'd love that." Pilar grinned as she walked away.

When Pilar arrived to clock in for work the next day,
she found another note instructing that she go to the
administration office.

"Good morning, Ms. Catrina."

"Good morning Pilar, have a seat. I'll be with you in just
a moment."

While waiting patiently, she read the newspaper articles
on the walls about the *BoJack Beer Distribution Company*.
Eventually, Catrina motioned for her to come into the office.

"Today, Mr. George sent me a message with instructions
to facilitate an orientation with you in the administration
office," she advised.

"Excuse me, why?" Pilar asked incredulously.

"A couple of days ago, Mr. George was reviewing profiles for our newest employees. When he came across yours, he was curious as to why you applied for a warehouse position. Well, when I mentioned your life plan and explained your long-term aspirations, he became quite intrigued. But more than this, he found you impressive and instructed me to groom and posture you for a position in the administration office. Pretty much, you get to start from the top, is what he told me. In fact, Mr. George wants you to start as soon as possible—today!"

"Wow, what an opportunity!" Pilar exclaimed while hesitating and looking down at her clothes.

"Would it be okay if I can start tomorrow? Honestly, what I'm wearing is not appropriate for an office setting."

"He thought you might say that."

Catrina opened the top drawer of her desk, pulled out an envelope, and handed it to Pilar. When she opened it, she saw a Platinum Visa card and asked, "What am I supposed to do with this?"

"It's the company credit card," Catrina explained. "You are to 'Go shop and don't stop,' in the words of Mr. George."

Devin walked into the office.

"Look who's here. Whispering in Pilar's ear, Catrina said, "Your chariot awaits you."

Devin leaned over and kissed Catrina's forehead. "Good morning, sister. Good morning, Pilar," he greeted.

Both ladies replied in concert, "Good morning, Devin."

Catrina advised Pilar that Devin would take her on the mandated shopping excursion. Pilar appeared somewhat taken aback and, at the same time, speechless. As Devin motioned her out of the office, he walked her to the car. When he opened the passenger door summoning her to get in—still perplexed—she couldn't determine if he had any interest in her or not.

"Okay, so where would you like to shop?"

Suddenly, she snapped out of it. "Here! I am not using this credit card. I will shop in my closet!" she said abruptly.

"My Closet? I've never heard of that department store. Where is it located?"

"My closet is in my apartment," she said snarkily.

As Pilar walked ahead of him, Devin asked, "Why not? I think Mr. G was very thoughtful."

"Really? How many other employees has Mr. Bojack been thoughtful to? Has he been this thoughtful to you? How much did you spend on your wardrobe using this platinum card, huh?"

Devin put his hands in his pockets and shook his head.

"He was generous enough to give me this platinum watch, but I don't know if he used that card in particular to purchase it."

Shoving the envelope and credit card into his chest, Pilar grudgingly got into the car and slammed the door. After being stuck in traffic for more than forty minutes, they finally arrived at her apartment. The ride should have only taken fifteen minutes. After getting out of the car, Pilar headed for her front door. Devin got out, leaned onto the car, and waited for her to change clothes. While waiting patiently, his phone rang.

After looking at the caller ID, Devin remarked, "Damn! It's Mr. G!" and he answered the phone.

"Good morning, Mr. G!"

"Devin."

"How's the weather, sir?"

Ignoring Devin's question, George asked, "How is my beautiful fiancée doing this morning?"

Removing the phone from his ear and looking at it as if he had seen a ghost, Devin mouthed to himself, surprisingly, "Fiancé?"

"Devin, are you there?"

"Yes, sir, I'm here. Where are you, if you don't mind me asking?"

"I'm sitting here in a cab waiting to be driven to the airport. By the way, I hope the process is going as well on your end as it is on mine."

"Yes, sir, it is. She can't wait until you return home."

"Really? Let me speak to her."

Telling a white lie, Devin said, "Well, she can't at this moment because she's inside the department store shopping."

"That's wonderful to hear! I wouldn't know what to say to her right now, anyway. I can't wait to lay my eyes on her. Devin?"

"Yes, sir?"

"Take a picture of her, send it to me, and then remove it from your phone," demanded George.

"Will do, sir."

At that moment, Pilar stepped out of her apartment and noticed Devin's reaction. He seemed mesmerized. Seemingly embarrassed, he immediately turned away and said to himself, "Stop! Stop right now!" Composing himself, he took a deep breath before turning back around to face Pilar. After helping her into the car, he couldn't help but notice how amazing she smelled. In a trance for what seemed like forever, he pulled himself together, jumped in the car, and drove off.

On the ride back to the company, the car was completely silent. When they pulled into the employee parking lot, Pilar could not hold her peace any longer.

After removing her seat belt, she faced Devin and asked, "I need to know, and I need to know right now. What is your problem with me?"

"I don't have a problem with you." She got out of the car, slammed the door, and walked away.

Catrina was sitting at her desk when Pilar walked into the administration office. "Girl, do you clean up nice! Did Devin take a second look?" she asked curiously.

Shaking her head, Pilar snapped, "Yes, no, I don't know—maybe!"

Another employee walked up and asked Catrina if he could speak with her.

"Sure, come on in. Pilar, give me just a moment."

The office door opened again, and this time it was Devin. When he looked at Pilar, she appeared obstinate. Still fuming about him downplaying her question, she immediately turned her back towards him.

After escorting the other employee out of the office, Catrina asked Pilar about the credit card.

"So, young lady, did you shop until you dropped?"

Removing the card from her purse, she handed it back to Catrina.

"I hope it won't offend Mr. Bojack, but I couldn't bring myself to use it. I don't think it's appropriate. Besides, what makes me so special to receive this kind of treatment?"

"My dear, I'm sure it won't bother him at all. However, if it were me, he wouldn't have to tell me twice," Catrina laughed out loud.

Devin knew he had to get back on Pilar's good side so that he could take her picture and send it to Mr. G., let alone try to convince her to go out with the boss man. He released a big sigh before asking, "Would you like to go out tonight and celebrate your new position?"

Pilar continued to ignore him. To get her attention, he cleared his throat loudly. "Excuse me?"

She looked at him out of the corner of her eye and replied, "I can't tonight; I have class."

Devin pulled out his phone and dialed Pilar's number. She answered it.

"What, Devin?"

"How about tomorrow night, and can you bring that beautiful smile of yours with you?"

"Maybe. I'll think about it."

She hung up and continued to ignore him. Devin then walked over to Catrina and asked if she knew when Mr. G. would return to the office.

"Not for four more days," she replied.

"Good," he said before he left and closed the door behind him.

CHAPTER 11

Much Love Daycare

George's flight arrived in Fort Wayne, Indiana, that afternoon. After picking up his car, he stopped by *Hawkins Fish House* to eat a plate of fried catfish and slaw before heading over to his sister Rachel's house, which is also her business, *Much Love Daycare*. When he arrived, he walked up to the door, not expecting to hear what he heard.

"I told you to make that snotty-nosed kid go lie back down with the rest of the brats," Rachel's boyfriend, Brick, screamed at her.

"Brick, he's hungry."

"Okay, so am I, and I eat first!"

Rachel tried to hold back tears of pain and resentment. "Brick, you need to leave right now," she pleaded.

"No, you put me out!"

"You know, I don't like this new you! If I had known you were this impatient—and an ass—when I met you six months ago, we wouldn't have gotten together.

Raising his hand to strike her, to Brick's surprise, he felt someone grab it in midair, lower it, and twist it behind his back. He was unaware that Rachel's brother, George, was standing behind him. When he tried to break free, he realized the grip was unbreakable, and with every attempt, he only intensified George's anger, worsening the pain. As Rachel began to cry while wiping away her tears, including her makeup, this was the moment George noticed that she had a black eye. His heart sunk instantly into the pit of his stomach.

"Did he do that to you?"

Saying nothing, she looked away. Looking on, the boy sitting at the table took a bite of his hotdog and nodded his head yes. George twisted Brick's arm even tighter, causing excruciating pain.

"You're breaking my arm!" Brick cried out.

"Do you hate women?" asked George.

"Nooooo!" Brick grunted in duress.

"Well, why does my sister have a black eye? What did she do to deserve this?"

"Nothing, man. I'm sorry!"

"Don't apologize to me, apologize to her, you piece of crap!"

Brick hesitated, forcing George to apply even more pressure.

"I'm sorry … I'm so, so sorry," he whimpered.

Stunned yet speechless, Rachel refused to accept his apology.

"Well, there you have it! Apology not accepted! Now, say goodbye!"

In a timid voice, Brick lowered his head and said softly, "Goodbye."

Still gripping Brick's arm, George escorted him to the front door and forcefully pushed him out of the house. Brick grabbed onto the railing to keep from stumbling down the steps and falling to the ground.

George stepped out on the porch and said, "You'll never bother my sister again, and that's a promise!"

When George walked back inside the house and into the kitchen, five other sad-faced children were sitting at the table.

"Would some good ole pizza put smiles on those tiny, sad faces?" he asked.

The children responded simultaneously, "Pizza, Pizza!"

George stretched out his hands, gesturing to Rachel to hug him. When she did, he gently embraced her, and she felt a sense of protection and peace in her brother's arms. He whispered in her ear, "No one is allowed to hit my big sister. If ever you feel unsafe and threatened in any way, remember that I'm only a phone call away. Got it?"

"I got it, little big brother," Rachel said softly.

George discreetly handed her some money.

"Hey, kiddos, what kind of pizza do you want?" asked George.

In concert, they shouted, "Pepperoni!"

"Okay, Ms. Rachel, pepperoni pizza it is!"

After telling his sister he had to leave, he headed towards the front door. He made sure to tell the kids that he hoped to see them another time.

Following close behind him, she said, "But wait, you just got here. Why are you leaving?"

"I've got some important things I need to handle. I'll be back soon."

He walked out onto the porch and shut the screen door between them. Turning back, he asked, "Rachel, what did you say Brick's last name is?"

She never said his last name and was curious to know why George was asking. However, she didn't question him and told him what he wanted to know. "His last name is Wricker, Brick Wricker."

George went onto Google and visited a website where he could pay to execute a thorough background check on Brick.

The time was approximately 2:00 a.m. when Brick woke up, startled and unable to move underneath the covers. Straddled over him, George held a jungle master machete above his head. Brick tried to shift in the bed and discovered that he couldn't move. Once his eyes focused, he realized George was on top of him.

He yelled, "Wait, wait, please! What are you doing?"

Using his other hand, George grabbed Brick's throat and put him in a chokehold. "Show me the hand you hit my sister with RIGHT NOW!"

Pinned down, Brick tried to break free but couldn't muster up enough strength. George tightened up his grip around Brick's neck and commanded him to show him that hand that gave his sister a black eye.

"Show me the hand, dammit."

"Man, I can't! I can't move.

George shifted, making it possible for Brick to comply.

"Now, raise it! Higher! Higher!"

Without zero hesitation, he whacked off that hand. After seeing his hand disconnect from his wrist and blood shoot across the room, Brick belted out a blood-curdling scream. George then ended his torture and choked him to death.

The following morning, before the children arrived, Rachel sat on her porch and sipped coffee, listening to birds chirp and sing. She felt free and rejuvenated. Reflecting on the one peaceful night she hadn't experienced in a long time since being in a relationship with Brick, she thought about how much longer she would have stayed in that situation if her brother did not show up when he did. But then again, she pondered about what she would do if Brick came back around. Suddenly, the small, yellow school bus pulled up, interrupting her thoughts. She walked down the driveway to greet her daycare kids, and after receiving a hug from each of them, she asked them to go inside and prepare to eat breakfast. After checking the mailbox and proceeding to walk back into the house herself, her next-door neighbor stepped onto her porch, holding a newspaper.

"Good morning, Rachel. I'm so sorry for your loss," the neighbor said.

Puzzled, Rachel asked, "Excuse me?"

"Your guy friend, Brick. Oh my God! You don't know?"

Rachel shook her head. "What are you talking about?"

"Oh, you poor thing. Brick was found dead last night."

Rachel's thoughts flashed back to when George was a little boy and when they were riding home on the bus from the pet shop. She remembered him telling her that he wasn't afraid to kill. When the neighbor abruptly called out her name, she snapped out of it.

"Rachel sweetheart, are you okay?"

Rachel inhaled, holding her breath for a few seconds. She then exhaled, took another deep breath, and replied, "I'm perfectly fine."

CHAPTER 12

The Atomic Bomb

When Devin pulled up to Pilar's apartment, she was waiting for him outside.

"Hey, Pilar, I hope I didn't make you wait too long."

"Hey, Devin, perfect timing. I just stepped out."

Tucking her hair behind her ear, she asked, "So, where are we headed tonight? Movies? Bowling? Skating?"

"No, the *Supper Club*. Jennie Cello is the featured artist this week. After supper, we can go next door to the *Atomic Bomb* and have a few drinks and maybe get on the dance floor."

"Yes, to the dance floor because I love to cut a rug. And, to Jennie Cello? It's an absolute YES!" she exclaimed. "She is awesome! The first time I had the pleasure of listening to her was at the Atlanta Airport. She caught my attention and had me at her first note. Many people stood around listening to her play and bobbed their heads to her beat."

At the Atomic Bomb, Devin ordered their drinks while Pilar went to the ladies' room. While walking back to the table, one of her favorite songs came on. Stepping onto the dance floor, she began to get her groove on and gestured for Devin to come and join her. After dancing to three fast songs, the DJ played a slow song. Devin tried to walk away, but Pilar took hold of his hand and pulled him in close to her. Finally, she was right where she wanted to be—in his arms. Laying her head on his shoulders and closing her eyes, she thought to herself, "Mmmm! He feels so good, and he smells delicious."

Devin allowed her to enjoy the moment. He was thinking, "Damn, Mr. G! Why must you have Pilar?"

When he looked up, he saw Mr. G standing there, one hand in his pocket, the other holding a drink. Abruptly, he pushed Pilar away and left the dance floor.

She followed him and asked, "Devin, what the hell was that? And why did you leave me standing there?"

As the waitress walked in their direction, he nervously replied, "I need a drink. How about you?"

"So, you left me standing there because you needed a drink?"

Picking up the glass, he drank his whiskey in two gulps.

"Pilar, didn't Catrina say that Mr. G. was returning in three or four days?"

"I think so. Why?"

"I could have sworn I saw him standing over there,"

Scanning the room, Pilar said, "Uh, I don't see Mr. George anywhere!"

Devin asked the bartender for more drinks. "I need three more of these, and bring her another one of what she's drinking."

"Thanks, but no thanks. I don't need another one. Someone has to be the responsible one," Pilar objected.

Devin became so intoxicated that she had to hold him up and walk him out of the bar. She leaned him up against the car to search his pockets for his car keys. He then reached for her hand.

Pilar said, "Oh, no, siree, absolutely not! You are in no condition to drive. Tonight, you are going to be chauffeured by me."

Instead of taking Devin home, Pilar took him to her apartment because she didn't want him to be alone. While struggling to get him from the car to the front door, he threw up.

"When you sober up, you're going to clean this up."

After finally getting him inside, Devin started to fall as she reached behind her to lock the door. With all her might, she lunged forward, grabbing him by the back of his shirt to keep him from falling and hitting the floor face first.

"Come on, now let's get you into the bathroom and clean up."

Devin stood over the toilet because he still felt like he had to throw up some more. Pilar looked in the half-empty medicine cabinet for something that might help soothe his stomach.

"I am sorry, Devin, but I don't have anything in here that's going to help you."

While tending to him, she could have sworn she heard someone at the front door but brushed it off. Unbeknownst to her, the front door knob did slowly turn, and the door opened quickly. George peeked into the apartment before quietly entering. He walked around the living room looking at Pilar's family photos when he heard her coming down the hallway. Stepping into a dark space, he hid in plain sight. Devin called out to Pilar.

"Hold on, Devin, I think I left the front door unlocked. Yep! I sure did."

After she locked the door, she heard a text message alert from her phone. She wondered if it was the professor dishing out another pop-up assignment. Before heading back to her room to grab her phone, she checked in on Devin and asked, "Are you okay in there?"

"I'm trying to be," replied Devin.

After she walked away, he received a text message. Grabbing his jacket off the sink, he took his phone out to read it. While biting his top lip, he hit the side of his right leg with his phone and grunted, "Damn, it's Mr. G. again.

"Pilar," he called out.

"Devin, is everything alright?" answering from the bedroom.

"Yes, I'm fine. Say, what do you think about Mr. G?"

"Uh, I don't!"

Thinking it was a perfect opportunity to express her feelings to him, she added, "But, I do think about you often."

Devin said quietly to himself, "No, no, no! This is not how it's supposed to go down. Mr. G. would kill me if he knew Pilar wanted me instead of him."

After turning on the water, he bent over the sink and splashed some on his face. When he stood up and looked in the mirror, Mr. G. was standing behind him. Fear instantly overcame him.

Angrily whispering in his ear, Mr. G. said, "She gave you the wrong answer, Devin," and then hit him in the head with one of Pilar's table statues he took from the living room.

When Pilar heard the loud thump, she rushed into the bathroom, only to find her boss standing over Devin, about to kick him. Realizing Devin was unconscious, she pushed him away and screamed, "What have you done, and what the hell are you doing in my apartment?"

He quickly did a balancing act to keep himself from falling into the toilet.

"Stay away from him," she cried.

Devin lay motionless on the floor, blood pouring from his head.

Screaming, Pilar cried out, "Help, help!"

Shouting over her, George said, "When I needed his help, he helped me alright. He helped himself to you!"

Pilar stood there frozen with a confused look on her face. Taking a deep breath, George calmed down but dramatically tried to explain what had just happened.

"Devin is who you might call my interceptor. He would introduce me to a female of my choosing, then eventually bring my name up in a conversation and ask her to go out on a date with me."

Shivering, with tears running down her cheeks, Pilar asked, "Is that why he kept bringing you up in our conversations?"

"Oh, so he did try to intercept you for me?"

Devin moaned.

Mr. G. grew angrier after losing Pilar's undivided attention when she shifted her focus entirely to Devin.

Kicking Devin viciously, George yelled, "He didn't try hard enough!"

Shifting from appearing shocked to angry, Pilar punched and scratched him in the face. After briefly struggling with him, George gained control and then put her in a chokehold, causing her to lose consciousness.

CHAPTER 13

Am I a Suspect?

The following morning, Devin was still lying in a pool of dried blood on Pilar's bathroom floor. His phone alarm went off, waking him up. As he tried to sit up, he grabbed his head, moaning. The pain he felt was excruciating. After sitting on the floor a few minutes longer, he realized where he was. He called out to Pilar before forcing himself to get up. Trying his best to move as quickly as he could around the apartment, frantically, he searched for her. Once he realized that she was not there, he called the police.

When two officers arrived and secured the apartment, Devin gave his statement to the lead officer, who called over the radio for the dispatcher to send a detective to their location. Upon arrival, the detective ordered the forensics expert, who came with him, to assess and evaluate what he deemed a crime scene. Meanwhile, he spoke with the officers about Devin's account of what happened. After learning that a kidnapping had possibly taken place, the detective dispatched the communications center to have an officer in the area report to the *Bojack Beer Distribution Company* and question George Bojack about the whereabouts of Pilar K'teace.

Devin sat on a stool as the EMT checked his vitals and the condition of his head. "Sir, I think you should let us take you to the hospital. These wounds require stitches."

"Can you put the stitches in right here, right now? Because I am not leaving unless I have to." Devin replied.

Once the detective finished speaking with the officers, he approached Devin and introduced himself. "Hey there, it's Devin, right?"

"Yeah, man, I'm Devin."

"Well, I'm sorry to meet you under these unfortunate circumstances, but can you tell what happened here?"

"What happened? Well, he hit me in the head and knocked me out!"

"Who hit you? The lady that lives in this apartment?"

"My answer has not changed from the first two times I was asked that question, and after I gave my statement." Irritated, Devin answered again, "No, it was George Bojack, the owner of *BoJack Beer Distribution Company*. He attacked me."

"Sure, it was," Detective Jenkins said smirkingly.

"What do you mean by sure it was?"

"I sent an officer to that business and the secretary told him that her boss has been out of town for nearly a week. She does not expect him back for another three to four days. So, can you tell me what really happened here?"

"So, you don't believe me? Am I a suspect?"

"Should you be?"

"No!" Devin yelled, "I told you exactly who did this!" His head started to bleed again.

"Once you patch him up, we're going for a ride to the station," the detective told the EMT.

"Pilar? Pilar?" George whispered, "Time to wake up, my sweet love."

He stroked her hair and softly kissed her ear while she sat on his bed between his straddled legs. Pilar slowly woke up and discovered that her hands and feet were tied together with zip ties and her mouth covered with duct tape. She began to mumble, but George couldn't understand what she was trying to say. He gently removed the duct tape.

She then yelled out, "Where the hell am I?"

"You're in your new home!" George said excitedly.

The voice sounded familiar to her. Compelled, she leaned back to turn and see who was sitting behind her. When she realized it was indeed Mr. George, she went crazy and frantically tried to get away.

Grabbing her by her arms and holding onto her tightly, he whispered, "Calm down, my love, I'm not going to hurt you."

She steeled herself, and George smiled gently.

"I would never, ever hurt you, so don't give me a reason to," he said cooingly, "You are the love of my life after all."

He turned his head slowly to kiss her ear again. Rejecting him, she shook her head and screamed out for help.

Laughingly, he said, "Scream as much as you want. I paid a lot of money for my home to be soundproof."

Meanwhile, Catrina showed up at George's house to water his plants. As she was standing at the kitchen sink filling the watering can, a scream she heard from upstairs startled her as no one should have been in the house while she was there. Catrina turned off the water, set the watering can on the counter, and immediately called 911. After she hung up the phone, she heard a man laughing, who sounded like Mr. George. Sneaking up the stairs and peeking into the master bedroom, to her amazement she saw a terrified Pilar in bondage.

"Why are you doing this to me?" Pilar cried out.

"Now, now. You are in a no-tears zone. So, no tears allowed, okay? Do you know what I'm thinking? One day, you're going to come around and love me just as much as I love you. I'm gentle, I'm caring, I'm respectful, and I love to share. Did you not receive your gift at the thrift store?"

Sickened by what she had just heard, Pilar asked, "So, you're the stalker?"

"No, I'm not a stalker, but I followed you into the department store, where you put on an amazing show. And, I even heard the conversation between you and the cashier about your spending allowance. So, the week afterward, I ordered Devin to make sure that the clothes you tried on were paid for in full and were waiting for you at the counter the next time you visited the thrift store. And, oh, I almost forgot, we never came up with a wedding date. What do you think about getting married on your birthday next year?"

Pilar was about to talk some serious sass to George. "Are you delusional? You must have lost your damn mind," she thought. But then she remembered she was tied up; she had to play along to survive.

"That sounds like a great plan," Pilar said, trying to sound excited.

"Good! It makes me happy that you agree," he said, hugging her tightly. "Now, I'm going to go and jump in the bathtub so that I can soak for a few minutes. My muscles are extremely sore this morning," he said, speaking casually.

George climbed out of bed and stood over Pilar. "You don't want to know what will happen if you try to leave, do you?"

He didn't wait for her to respond and walked away.

Catrina noticed that George's bathroom was situated adjacent to the bedroom. When he entered the bathroom, she quietly stepped into the doorway of his bedroom.

As her eyes filled with tears, Pilar was elated to see Catrina and whispered, "Catrina, please, help me!"

"Pilar, what on earth is going on here?"

"Girl, Mr. George is crazy. He is demanding that I marry him. But, wait? How the heck did I even get here? Did he kidnap me? He had to have kidnapped me because why are my hands and feet zip-tied? He must be out of his mind to think I would marry him after doing all this to me. And, where is Devin?"

When they heard him coming, Catrina rushed back out into the hallway to find someplace to hide.

"Wait! Please, don't leave me," whispered Pilar.

Catrina looked back and mouthed, "Girl, I'm not going to leave you," and then gestured for her to be quiet.

George entered the bedroom with a curious look on his face. "Pilar, my love, who are you talking to?"

"No one."

Becoming impatient with her, accusingly, he inquired again, "No one, really?"

Her stomach growled noisily. "I was talking to my belly."

He walked over to her, placed his hand on her stomach, and giggled. "Yeah, that was quite loud. You should've told me you were hungry. How about a bowl of cereal?"

She looked at him and shrugged her shoulders but knew when he left that she and Catrina would need more time to try and escape.

"I don't like cereal, hot or cold."

"Will pancakes, sausages, and eggs do?"

"Sure. Can I have a large glass of fresh-squeezed OJ with that, too?"

"Of course, sweetie. Anything for my fiancé."

Pilar flashed him a phony grin as he turned to walk away.

After Catrina heard him run downstairs, she waited a few seconds before going back into the master bedroom.

"Girl, I was hiding in the hall closet, and oh my goodness, I saw the most expensive towels I've ever seen in my life."

Annoyed, Pilar demanded Catrina to focus on the matter at hand and call the police. "Catrina, are you serious right now? Please call the police!"

"The police should be on the way. When I heard you scream earlier, I called them immediately."

"Okay, good. Now, please untie me already!"

Attempting to break the zip ties as fast as she could, she struggled to remove them. "Why are these things so hard to get off?

Look for some scissors," commanded Pilar.

Catrina opened the nightstand drawer, and inside was Pilar's cell phone. Meanwhile, as George searched the cabinets for the ingredients he needed to make pancakes, he noticed the pitcher full of water on the counter. He then realized that Catrina was in the house and ran back upstairs.

"Grab my phone and hide it under the pillow."

Catrina hurriedly hid the phone under the pillow and continued rummaging around in the drawer. "Pilar, I don't see any scissors here. Let me check the other nightstand."

When she turned around, Pilar looked up, and there George stood at the edge of the bed. Catrina squealed and grabbed her chest. "Mr. George!" she said surprisingly.

"Why, it's good to see you, Ms. Catrina," he replied while resting his hand on her shoulder, "Thank you so much for watering my flowers."

Nervously, she said, "You're welcome, sir," while trying to walk past him.

He wasted no time to tase her, and she dropped to the floor instantly.

Pilar screamed hysterically and cried out, "Mr. George, please don't, please don't hurt her!"

"What just happened here is all your fault because you lied when I asked who you were talking to."

He grabbed Catrina by the wrists and dragged her into the bathroom.

Pilar sobbed uncontrollably and asked him, "What are you going to do to her?"

Once he made it into the bathroom, she reached under the pillow, grabbed her cell phone, and texted Devin.

CHAPTER 14

Take That Back

Devin was being escorted out of Pilar's apartment when he received her text.

"Excuse me, Mr. Detective. That text tone belongs to Pilar. Can I check it, please?" asked Devin.

Detective Jenkins gave him a doubtful look.

"I'm telling you, man; she's texting me."

He checked Devin's phone and read the text:

HELP! MR. GEORGE'S HOUSE!

The detective uncuffed Devin and ordered the officers on duty to head over to Mr. Bojack's residence to investigate the text. Before they left, he dispatched the command center to request the address. He learned that there were officers already en route to that exact location. Devin anxiously begged them to hurry and get there as quickly as possible.

"Please, detective. You are using lights and sirens. I mean, the man tried to kill me, and I'm afraid that if she doesn't do what he tells her to do or follow his instructions, he'll try to kill her, too."

"Don't worry. George Bojack's residence is not too far away from here. With lights and sirens, we're about 12 minutes away," explained the detective, "Now, put on your seatbelt.

In the bathroom, George dunked Catrina's head into the tub filled with water. "I hate to do this to you, sweetheart, but I need you to say goodbye RIGHT NOW!"

Every time he brought her up for air, he demanded she say the word. Already exhausted after holding her breath for so long, gasping, she tried her best not to drown.

"No, I won't say it! I won't!"

As George was about to dunk her head again, Pilar got out of the bed and hopped over to the bathroom entryway to see what she could do to help Catrina. Suddenly, there was a loud knock at the front door, followed by the doorbell ringing repeatedly. While hopping away and screaming for help, Pilar tripped and fell onto the bedroom floor. After putting Catrina into a headlock and knocking her unconscious, George dropped her to the floor and rushed back into the bedroom. He then snatched Pilar up off the floor and threw her back onto the bed.

"If I trusted you, I wouldn't have to do this again," he told her while covering her mouth with another piece of tape, "Now, don't budge."

The doorbell rang again and again. "Coming!" George shouted. He ran down the stairs and peeked out the window. After gaining his composure, he calmly opened the door.

"How can I help you, officers?"

"We received a call about someone screaming for help in this house."

A moment later, Detective Jenkins pulled up. He advised the first officers on scene to standby and that he would take it from there.

"Hello, Mr. Bojack, my name is Detective Jenkins. We first received a call about a woman screaming in this house. We then received a suspicious text message directing us to your address. We suspect that the text came from the same person. May we come in and have a look around, sir?" asked the detective.

"Uhhh, no, sir," said George, "I assure you that that won't be necessary. I'm here all alone. My fiancée Pilar is out shopping."

Devin stepped out from behind Detective Jenkins and shouted, "She is not your fiancé!"

George was outraged and reached for Devin's neck. "You traitor! I should have killed you when I had the chance!"

The police intervened and stopped him from attacking Devin. An officer immediately handcuffed George and placed him in the back of the police car.

Devin stepped through the doorway and called out, "Pilar! Pilar!"

Pilar realized Mr. George taped her hands in front of her, so she yanked the tape from her mouth and screamed, "Devin! I'm up here!"

The police pushed past him with their guns drawn and began to search and clear the downstairs for any immediate danger. Detective Jenkins instructed Devin to wait outside and proceeded upstairs to rescue Pilar. Pilar wondered why it was taking Devin so long to get to her, so she jumped out the bed, hopped over to the door, and opened it—and there stood Detective Jenkins and two of the officers.

The detective grabbed her and pulled her out of the bedroom before whispering, "Are you Pilar K'teace?

Shaking her head dramatically, she replied, "Yes, yes, I am!"

"Is there anyone else here?"

"Oh my God, YES! Please help Catrina! She could be dead! That bastard tased her, dragged her into the bathroom, and repeatedly dunked her head in the bathtub filled with water," she explained.

Detective Jenkins gestured to one of the officers to remove the zip ties from Pilar's wrists and feet and escort her downstairs and out of the house. He then directed the other officer to assist him with helping and possibly saving Catrina. After all, they didn't hear a sound coming from the bathroom. When they found her, she lay sprawled across the floor unconscious. After kneeling on the floor, the detective lifted her head, and she slowly began to gain consciousness. When she opened her eyes, she cried hysterically, fighting to get away.

"Calm down, Catrina. We're here to help you. Don't worry, you're safe now," said the officer. He then radioed to ask for the medic on the scene to come to her aid.

Outside, Devin was relieved to see that Pilar was safe.

"Pilar!" he yelled!

Pilar ignored him and walked over to the squad car that George was sitting in. The window was halfway down. An officer kept her from getting too close.

"You bastard! I hate you with a passion!" she screamed.

"Pilar, please do not talk like that, my love," begged George.

"You fool, are you out of your mind?! I will never be yours! Goodbye, George, *goodbye!*"

George became so enraged to the point that his eyes turned bloodshot. "Take that back," he warned, "and say, see you later!"

Giggling under her breath, Pilar said, teasingly, "*Goodbye!*"

Turning her back on George, she walked over to Devin and slapped him in the face. Unfortunately, the police didn't see the attack coming and restrained her a bit too late.

Devin hung his head, "Please, let her go. I deserved that and whatever else she might want to do to me."

The police released her without hesitation. One officer said to the other, "Was this not an eventful evening. Aren't you glad you decided not to call out tonight?"

They smirked at each other and shifted their attention back to Devin and Pilar to diffuse any further commotion.

"That maniac told me everything," Pilar retorted.

"Please don't be mad at me," Devin begged.

"Why would I be mad? You were only doing your job. To be perfectly honest, I'm mad at myself. While you were trying to hook me up with that psychopath, I found myself falling for you day by day. My soul yearned for YOU, and I placed YOU in my heart. I thought that at some point, you would catch my vibes and respond and act accordingly. But no, YOU were too focused on completing that pervert's mission. And now, I must begin and endure the painful process of purging YOU," she explained.

Crossing her arms, she looked away and started to cry.

Devin began to apologize profusely and asked Pilar to forgive him.

"Pilar, I am sincerely sorry! I had no idea that he would go to this extreme to be with you. Believe me; I didn't."

"Just leave me alone," she replied.

Devin moved closer to her and tried to explain himself again.

"Pilar, let me help you understand. I did catch your vibe, but I had no choice but to ignore your advances for the sake of protecting myself and my job. Mr. George can be tough at times, but I truly didn't know he was capable of doing something like this."

Tapping her on the chest near her heart, he said, "Please don't purge me. Trust me! I want you just as much as you want me."

She jumped into his arms, wrapped her legs around his waist, and they locked lips and kissed each other passionately. The taste of Devin's lips was everything she had expected.

George became infuriated and couldn't believe what was happening right before his eyes. Like a toddler, he had a tantrum and began kicking the door from the inside of the police car. He shouted, "Get away from her, you asshole! I'm warning you! Get the hell away from her!"

"Stop kicking the door, Mr. Bojack, or we will tase you," shouted one of the police officers, "You'll also be charged with vandalizing police property."

After being warned, George cringed his teeth, took a couple of deep breaths, and looked at the officer with contempt. He ignored the warning, slowly raised both his legs and with his feet, he forcefully kicked out the glass on the back passenger window. The sound of the shattering glass interrupted Pilar and Devin's moment of bliss. Flabbergasted, they looked on in disbelief at what was happening. They couldn't believe that this was their boss behaving like a maniac. The advising officer followed through with his promise and tased him. Unfortunately, being tased didn't faze him, requiring the other officers at the scene to intervene. When they realized that they had a monster on their hands, the takedown training they learned at the police academy went out the window. They proceeded to employ street-like tactics that caused the supervising officer to look the other way, who quickly realized he needed to control what was becoming a dangerous situation.

"Guys, shackle the man's feet and hitch the shackles to the harness at the bottom of the seat so he won't be able to move," commanded the supervisor.

After course correcting and securing George in the car, they all seemed to be out of breath.

Pilar and Devin's attention shifted when they noticed the EMTs and Detective Jenkins escorting Catrina out of the house. They both ran over to check on her.

"Catrina, my God, are you okay? Are you hurt anywhere?" Pilar asked while grabbing and hugging her tightly.

"Sis, are you good?" asked Devin. "That fool better be glad the police are standing between us."

"I'll be okay," responded Catrina.

Being snatched out of his home, placed in handcuffs, and thrown into the back of a police car resulted in George having a nervous breakdown. Already challenged mentally, seeing Devin and Pilar kissing is the reason why he snapped and lost it, only exacerbating his condition of which he had zero self-awareness. His head began twitching to the left, and his right eye wouldn't stop blinking. After being tased, he drifted into a memory of when he was an eight-year-old boy, jumping on a trampoline and playing with two of his friends.

His mom stepped out of their house, calling him in for lunch. "George, it's lunchtime!"

He yelled back, "I'm coming, Mom!" running to her with a gigantic smile on his face.

One of his friends yelled out to him, "Goodbye, George!"

George turned around and waved. "Goodbye!"

Kneeling in front of him, his mother kindly reminded him, "Mommy told you never say *goodbye* to anyone, right? Saying *goodbye* could mean over, done, final, never again. You're supposed to say, *see you later*. It comes with another chance that you might see that person in the future."

George's thoughts jumped from that moment to when his mother was lying in a hospital bed as he stood by her side.

Struggling and gasping for air between each word, she said, "George ... baby ... this ... is ... goodbye...."

Frightened and trembling, he replied, "No, Mommy, not goodbye. You mean *see you later* right?"

A nurse stood next to him, clutching him, to keep him from climbing into the hospital bed.

In her last breath, his mother said, "Goodbye, George."

"Mommy? Mommy?" he called out and cried.

CHAPTER 15

Released

In a non-emergency ambulance, George was lying on a gurney with one of his hands cuffed to a rail. From head to toe, a white sheet covered him. He was still calling for his mommy when the ambulance pulled up to the *Wilson Center*. The driver looked back at George through the rearview mirror. His co-worker was sitting in the front passenger seat, who then unbuckled his seat belt, climbed to the back of the ambulance, and pulled the sheet back, uncovering George's face.

"Mr. Bojack, after all the crap you've done, don't you think it's a little too late to be calling on your mommy?"

He pulled the cover back over George's face, only to remove it again. "Oh, and by the way, welcome to the *Wilson Center for the Mentally Ill*: the crazy house, the loony bin."

George pulled the covers back over his face with his free hand.

Looking at the monitor, a security guard noticed an EMT pushing a gurney up to the indoor. She buzzed him in. Excited to see a familiar face, he asked, "Hey, lady! How long have you been working in this lovely establishment?"

"Well, today is my third day of orientation," she replied.

"Oh, really? And they got you holding down the post by yourself already?"

"Unfortunately, yes! They are short-staffed, and it's like that everywhere now.

The other EMT who drove the ambulance interrupted their conversation when he rang the doorbell, prompting them both to look at the monitor.

"Oh, you can let that funny-faced dude in; he's my partner."

The security guard buzzed him in.

"Alright, we need to check this guy in and leave because dispatch wants us to arrive at our next pickup within forty-five minutes," explained the driver.

The security guard never pulled the sheet back to look at George's face before the EMTs rolled him over to the intake door. After pushing the button to buzz them in, the driver handed the patient file to the processor, who quickly perused through it.

"Now, who do we have here? And why the gurney?" asked the processor.

Pulling the sheet back from George's face, the driver said, "His name is George Bojack. When the judge sentenced him to this facility indefinitely, and then to the *J. Henry Maximum State Prison* for twenty-five years, for kidnapping and attempted murder, he refused to get up and walk."

The processor keyed George's information into the computer.

"Can you sign the release forms, please? We have to get out of here and head to our next pickup," the EMT stated.

"Sure, give me a second," replied the processor.

"Our next transport is in a wheelchair, so we will come back to pick up the gurney at the end of our shift."

She signed the forms and buzzed them out.

Another prisoner named Jackson Archer was wearing a green tee-shirt with the word RELEASE on the back of it. Before signing his final paperwork to be released from the facility, the processor instructed him to have a seat while she finished the intake paperwork for their new patient. After swinging a bag that contained his personal belongings back and forth for nearly ten minutes, Jackson stood up and asked, "Excuse me, miss, can you move faster and wave that magic wand of yours and let me up out of this joint?"

"Can you have a seat, as I instructed you, and wait your turn, please? I'll be with you just as soon as I finish," she replied.

Under his breath, Jackson called her a heffa. He then asked, "Do you mind if I go to the bathroom?"

"Go right ahead, Mr. Archer."

After he went into the bathroom, the processor answered the ringing phone.

"Hello, Processing! ... Yes, I want to sing happy birthday to her, too! ... Yes, I have an intake, but he's on a gurney and can't walk. ... Okay, I am coming right now. Mr. Archer will be okay to wait another five minutes."

She hung up the phone and cracked open the door to the men's bathroom. "Mr. Archer, I need to step away from my desk for a moment. I'll be right back. Stay put, okay?"

"Whoa, whoa, whoa, wait a minute. How long is right back, miss?" he asked.

"I'll be gone no more than five minutes tops."

"Alright! You got five minutes and no longer. I'm ready to go!" he said after flushing the toilet.

As soon as the processor let herself out, George got up from the gurney and went into the bathroom, only to find Jackson washing his hands and whistling.

"You're such a jolly gentleman," remarked George.

Jackson turned the water off and grabbed a couple of paper towels to dry his hands.

"Man, I've been in this hellhole for five long years. I'm ready to get up out of here and go buy me a bottle of booze and boobs," he explained.

"Good for you," replied George. Jackson tossed the paper towel into the trash and headed toward the door.

Giving him a cunning look, George said, "See you later."

Jackson asked, "Don't you mean goodbye?"

When the processor returned, she finished George's paperwork. "Alright, Mr. Bojack. Once you pass through these doors, the doctor will examine you. After your exam, you'll go to room 525 on the fifth floor, where you'll reside until you transition to the prison."

She then made a phone call. "I have one for pickup, and please bring a gurney. Thank you." She hung the phone and looked over at the gurney.

"Okay, sir. Before they come to retrieve you, do you have any questions?"

After waiting for a response and no answer, with an attitude, she said, "Mr. Bojack, they said you could not walk; they did not say you could not talk."

She pulled the sheet back only to find Mr. Archer lying on the gurney—dead. She quickly called for help over the intercom system before going to search for George in the bathroom. An alarm abruptly sounded off throughout the building.

After masterminding his breakout at the mental institution, George walked as calmly as possible, trying his best not to draw attention to himself. Every step he took away from the building was more powerful and hopeful.

"You're a genius, George, beautiful escape," he muttered to himself.

He then noticed two male employees who looked as if they were returning from lunch; they were carrying doggie bags and beverages. As the workers walked past George, one of them remarked, "Hey, congratulations on your release!" causing him to freeze in place.

"You have a release shirt on, man," the worker said, "You're good. Take a deep breath."

George couldn't help but let out a sigh of relief.

The other worker said, "I've worked on every floor in this building, and honestly, I don't remember you at all."

Stepping towards George, he asked, "What floor were you on?"

Immediately, George feared being captured and began to mumble, "I'm, uh, uhm, uhm…."

"Wh … What are you saying?" asked the worker, "I can't understand you."

George held his head down and began to shiver frantically.

"Dude, why are you nervous all of a sudden? Better yet, let's go back inside the building…."

Before he could utter another word, George took off, running as fast as he could.

"Yo, come back here!" the worker commanded, looking stunned at his coworker. "Why did he take off running? I was just kidding."

His coworker replied, "If you stepped to me like that on my release date, I would've taken off running, too!"

They both giggled and went back to work. Coincidentally, when the workers stepped into the building, the alarm went off.

CHAPTER 16

Delta 88

George was determined to keep running until he found a safe place to hide or until he dropped dead from exhaustion. His chest hurt, and his body tensed up after overworking his muscles. He could feel the sweat beading up across his forehead before it rolled down his face and into his eyes, stinging them. He ran into an alley about ten blocks away from the crazy house and lucked out. Out of breath, he leaned against the building to hold himself up. After catching his breath, he tiptoed around the garage, peeking through the broken windows to make sure no one else was occupying the space. When he gained access, he positioned himself and sat where he could see every entry— both doors and all three windows. He felt safe there for the moment and was able to relax.

After dozing off to sleep, the sound of police sirens and barking woke him up. He jumped up and realized that he needed to figure out how to change his scent to trick and throw off the dogs. Poking his head outside, he checked to see if anyone was out there looking for him. No one was there, so he exited the garage and took off, running further up the alley.

While running, George noticed two trash cans filled to the brim. He thought it was a good idea to put the garbage on himself to cover his scent. When he ripped open the bags and dumped the contents onto the ground, he couldn't help but gag because the smell was so awful. The bag contained dirty diapers and spoiled-rotten food. He knew if he stood there and thought about what to do, he wouldn't go through with it. So, without second-guessing himself, he took a deep breath and proceeded to lie down and roll around in the pile of trash. The stench was overwhelming. Still gagging, he thought if that was what it would take to keep the dogs off, so be it.

After pulling and peeling off some of the nasty trash that stuck to him, he tossed everything to the ground and took off running again down the alley until he saw Jerry's Junk Yard across the road. The junkyard housed plenty of broken-down cars he could hide in, possibly, for a day or two. Hoping to find food while there, he prayed he wouldn't starve to death if he didn't.

The only thing that stood between George and the junkyard was a fence approximately ten feet high. He felt a tiny stroke of luck when he discovered a hole in the wire fence covered by bushes. Once he crawled through the hole, he spotted a car his mother used to own, a 1994 maroon Delta 88 Oldsmobile with tinted windows. It was as if the car was calling out to him, "Come to me, and I will protect you."

George was about to open the front passenger door but hesitated and opened the back door instead. He then got in. After shutting the door, a German Rottweiler with a massive head jumped onto the trunk, barking aggressively. He thought he was captured and done for, for good.

As he was about to open the door and surrender peacefully, he heard a man yell out, "Bruiser, get down from there and stop all that barking! You're giving me a headache."

Taking his hand off the door handle, George slowly laid down on the floor of the car. Bruiser ignored the command and continued to bark.

"Shut up, you stupid damn dog," the man snapped as he picked up a rock and threw it toward Bruiser.

The dog jumped off the trunk of the car and paced back and forth, growling. George remained still, thinking if he did, the dog would go away. However, he had no choice but to move because he felt some tingling in his left foot, most likely from a lack of blood circulation. He thought the perfect opportunity came when he heard the junkyard man using a drill to remove a part from another car parked next to the Oldsmobile. He believed that the sound would smother out any noise he might make. He took a chance and shifted his body to allow blood to flow through his foot, causing the car to move slightly. Standing on his hind legs, Bruiser started barking hysterically and pounced on the back-passenger window with his front paws. After the junkyard man finished working on the car, he walked over and grabbed Bruiser by his collar.

"Dog, look, I've had about enough of you and your barking, and, since you choose not to listen, you're sleeping in the cage tonight!" he yelled angrily.

Bruiser tried to pull away, but his grip was too tight. George lifted his head slightly to see if the coast was clear, and it was. Again, he felt a bit of relief and sighed. His thoughts overwhelmed him.

Where am I? When was the last time I ate? Where can I get money to buy a phone? Who can I or should I call to help me? What about transportation? And how do I take a bath and change clothes?

He then remembered he was far west, near the edge of the city. He needed to head east to make his way to the tiny house in the woods situated about a mile off the nearest road. That house stashed anything he would ever need. He could barely keep his eyes open but also couldn't go to sleep. He managed to stay awake a bit longer and reminisced about the tiny house.

CHAPTER 17

Twist of Fate

About a year before, at one of his monthly manager meetings, George overheard a conversation his managers had while waiting for Catrina to arrive with the agenda.

"Has anyone seen Todd?" asked one of the employees.

"Is he that homeless guy who has been hanging around for years?" asked another one.

"Yes, I saw him two weeks ago, over near the *Taylor Street Festival*." A female manager replied. "I asked him if he was okay because he looked extremely ill. Hesitating, he eventually said no but explained that he went to the free clinic to receive treatment for dehydration a few days prior. After having his blood drawn for testing, the doctor informed him that his white blood cell count was severely low and his vitamin D level was extremely high. He said to me, 'I think I'm dying.' I asked him what made him feel like he was dying. He told me that the doctor wanted to test him for Leukemia and colorectal cancer, but he told them not to bother and got up and left. When he shared this news with me, my heart hurt for him. Even right now, I feel so sorry for him because I don't know how he's doing. Poor guy! He said his only regret was not experiencing the American dream, owning his own home, finding a wife, and having a couple of knuckleheads."

A slight burst of laughter cut through the silence as she finished telling everyone what she knew about Todd. She went on to explain further.

I asked him if he would consider changing his mind about finding out what's really going on and receiving treatment. I told him that at least knowing would be the difference between him living and dying. He looked up into the sky, and a slight grin came over his face. He said, 'No. I want to see what comes next. To do so, I must give up my space here on earth. Hopefully, the one who comes in behind me has a better life, not that mine was all that bad, just somewhat unconventional.' He said his final wish was that he hoped he would not take his last breath asleep in a gutter."

The story about the homeless guy stayed in George's subconscious the entire day, to the point of tossing and turning as he tried to sleep through the night. Around 2:00 a.m., he let out a loud grunt before pushing his blanket to the side and sitting on the edge of his bed.

"Why can't I get this story out of my brain?" he asked himself while tapping his pointer finger against his head a few times. Suddenly, a light bulb turned on.

"He wants a house!"

George jumped up and grabbed the first pieces of clothing he saw and put them on, not caring if they were pressed or even clean. He was on a mission and rushed out the front door. Before backing into the street from his driveway, he stopped the car and searched for his phone to text his driver, Devin.

"Cancel my pickup for this morning. I'll contact you later today if I need your services," George told Devin.

Driving around his company, scoping the area out for an hour, he searched for Todd to no avail. When he felt sleepy, he drove a few blocks over to an all-night diner to grab a cup of coffee. Coincidentally, when he pulled up in his Lexus, he noticed Todd pushing his cart filled with his belongings into the parking lot, heading towards the restaurant.

After parking his cart on the side of the building, Todd immediately ran into the restroom located outside the diner to take a leak. After exiting, he noticed a man leaning up against a nice luxury car, possibly waiting for him to come out of the restroom. Suddenly, the man started walking towards him.

"Good morning, Todd," greeted George.

"Good morning," Todd replied before looking to see who he had greeted. He gasped and became extremely surprised when he recognized who it was.

"Mr. George?" Todd greeted him formally.

"Yes!" George replied.

Todd was thrilled to know that a man of his status acknowledged him and knew his name. As a side thought, he wondered if Mr. George was waiting to use the outside restroom.

"Excuse me, sir, if you're planning on going in there, I absolutely would not if I were you. The diner allows homeless people to use that restroom, and it doesn't have golden Mac faucets or Toto toilets either. It's the total opposite experience of what I'm assuming you're used to—believe me," explained Todd.

Since Todd mentioned the faucet and the toilet, George thought it was the perfect segue to the conversation he wanted to have with him. Smiling, he asked, "How about breakfast and coffee?"

Patting his pockets, Todd asked, "Why would you want to break bread with a homeless guy like me?"

George kept his answer simple. "Why would I not?"

Todd obliged.

George leading the way, both men walked into the restaurant and sat in a booth nearest the door. After the waitress took their order, they engaged in small chit-chat. Upon receiving their food, George sipped on his cup of black coffee and watched Todd take small bites of his breakfast.

"I haven't eaten a feast of this magnitude in years. If I had the means, I'd cook breakfast every morning!"

"Means?" asked George.

"You know, a crib of my own," Todd clarified.

George smirked, asking, "A crib with golden Mac faucets and Toto toilets?"

Todd's face turned red with embarrassment, appearing to become uncomfortable.

To make him feel more at ease, George said, jokingly, "No matter the name of the faucets and toilets, they all produce the same outcome."

Todd smiled. "True!"

George reared back in his chair and concurred with Todd. "True indeed, it's not the brand names that matter!"

"So, tell me, Todd, what would the interior of a beautiful home look like to you?"

"Oh, you do not want to open that can of worms, Mr. George."

"Yes, I do."

A huge smile came over Todd's face.

"Hold that thought; I'll be right back."

He went outside to search his cart, looking for a folder. "Found it!" he said to himself.

After sitting back down, Todd opened his folder and scattered pictures of furniture ideas for an entire house across the table. He talked at great length about why he chose his color scheme, his window treatment, the deck he would have built, and his home's curb appeal. George listened to every detail before releasing a yawn.

"Excuse me, my apologies. I didn't mean to bore you."

"No, you didn't. I didn't sleep well or long enough last night. But I find your pictures remarkably interesting. Thank you for showing them to me."

Todd gathered up his pictures and placed them back into the folder. "Mr. George, thanks for treating me to breakfast. I need to go now so that I can claim my spot on the street before someone else takes it."

"Wait, Todd, I need to be honest with you."

Todd hesitated before giving George the go-ahead nod.

"Last night, I had a hard time sleeping because of a conversation I overheard my employees having about you and your illness. Are you sure you do not want treatment?"

George's concern stunned Todd. Replying sarcastically, he asked, "Thoughts about me caused you to have insomnia? But why, sir?"

"Well, we're deeply concerned about you."

"Really?"

"Really, and I can prove to you my sincerity."

"Ok, I'm listening."

"No one knows this but Ms. Catrina and me, but in my office is an envelope with your name on it that has a stack of tens in it. I instructed her to give you one every Friday for a job well done!"

"Sir, I don't quite understand?"

"The thing is this. You don't just hang out to panhandle on my company property. I notice that you're there after hours picking up trash and other debris. I appreciate that more than you know because you don't have to do that. Tears filled Todd's eyes, knowing that he was worth something to someone. He had no idea that anyone ever cared, especially George.

"Alright, Todd. Let's make a deal. Meet me back at this diner in three days, but not so early. Let's say we meet at 7:00 am. Deal?"

Again, Todd was amazed that George extended his hand. As he shook it, he smiled. "I appreciate you for appreciating me, Mr. George."

George smiled back at Todd with a nod of approval. "Todd, all I ask is that you keep this meeting between us confidential. You can't even tell your girlfriend."

Instantly, a frown fell upon Todd's face. "I get it! You don't want your friends to know you hang out with a bum," he said sadly.

"No! That is not true. I do not want you to say anything because if my employees and others find out that we've been hanging out, they might stop being so generous to you, and I don't want them to treat you any differently."

Staring at the ground, Todd agreed and acknowledged that what George said made sense and vowed not to utter a word about meeting up with him. He told George this story about his ex-girlfriend, explaining that she left him for another homeless guy when she found out how sick he was. Following George to his car, Todd watched him pull out of the parking lot. He held onto his breakfast as long as he could before regurgitating it, which was all he seemed to do lately, hoping that no one saw him barf. But, unbeknownst to him, George saw him through his rearview mirror. After noticing Todd slumped over his cart, he put his car in reverse to go back and check on him. When he got out of the car, he saw that Todd was grey and could barely stand or hold himself up.

"Hey, man, can I take you to the ER?" asked George.

Although Todd refused, George didn't feel good about leaving him there and offered to put him up in a motel outside the city limits. Todd agreed.

"I would be all alone way out there by myself, though."

Reassuring him, George said, "Todd, you'll have everything you need and want. I promise you that."

"What about my cart?"

"I'll put everything in your cart into my trunk."

George helped Todd get into the back seat of the car so that he could lie down, and as promised, he stored his belongings in the trunk, except for the folder, which he tossed in the front passenger seat. He paid for Todd to stay at the hotel for five days while completing his plans and hoping he wouldn't die anytime soon. George offered the clerk a thousand dollars in cash to keep a close eye on him and asked her to make sure Todd drank plenty of broth and water. He gave her a little extra for anything else Todd might need.

"No matter what, no matter how sick he gets, do not call the ambulance because he will refuse to go to the hospital. My number is on his information sheet if you need me, " George instructed the clerk.

Before unloading Todd's belongings out of his trunk, he assisted him out of the car to help him into the motel room. After pulling back the covers on the bed, he then helped Todd lie down.

"Mr. George, I think I should clean up before I lie down underneath those lovely, fresh sheets.

"Are you strong enough to take a shower?"

"I believe so. I gained a little strength when I took a nap on the way here."

After taking a nice, long hot shower, Todd climbed into the bed and instantly fell asleep. Before leaving, George woke him up and encouraged him to stay in the room unless he had an emergency.

"Hey, buddy, tomorrow you'll have everything you need as promised—new clothes, food, and even b12 and one-a-day vitamins. You'll have absolutely no reason to leave this room. I need you to rest and focus on gaining back your strength. Deal?" Todd agreed to cooperate and fell back to sleep. George whispered and said, "See you later, my friend."

CHAPTER 18

Curb Appeal

The time came for Todd to check out of the motel room. He had to be out by noon. He waved as George was driving into the parking lot to pick him up.

"Good afternoon, Mr. George."

"Good afternoon, Todd."

George popped the trunk so that Todd could load his belongings. As they drove away from the motel, Todd asked sarcastically, "Where to now, Mr. George, back to the streets?"

George smirked at him and kept driving.

Todd turned around in his seat and looked out the back window. "Excuse me, sir, but where are we going? The city is back the other way."

"I need to take care of some business before we go back into city."

Shrugging his shoulders, Todd replied, "Ok."

George drove for about ten minutes until they came upon a wooded area with a long driveway that led to a tiny house. Todd's face lit up with wonder and excitement. He instantly became mesmerized by the cute little house and its curb appeal.

"WOW! This place reminds me of the pictures I showed you from my folder…."

Before Todd could say another word, George placed a key in his hand.

Todd looked at the house key and held it to his chest, and screamed, "NO! Are you serious? Is this for me?"

George nodded. "Yes, for you!"

Todd was about to jump out of the car when George grabbed him by the arm and said, "Under one stipulation. "

"I'm listening, Mr. George."

Giving him a stern and authoritative look, George said, adamantly, "No one is to know about this house, and I mean no one! You got that?"

Without responding, Todd pulled away from him and ran up to the front door. He was ecstatic! Calming himself by taking a long, deep breath before putting the key into the hole to open the door, he slowly opened the door and peeked inside. He couldn't believe his eyes and almost became frozen. He pushed the door open, walked in, and did a complete 360-degree turn while inhaling the fresh smell of what luxury is and feels like. The interior was gorgeous and all that he had envisioned. Everything smelled and looked brand new, the furniture, the hardwood floors, and the color scheme throughout. Todd took off running to the bathroom and was stopped in his tracks by what he discovered, a Toto toilet and a golden Mac faucet sink.

He said to himself, "My goodness, look at that beautiful sink and toilet. I just cannot believe this."

The newness, lavishness, and immaculacy of the tiny house filled his soul with joy and completion.

When Todd heard George entering the house, he walked out of the bathroom slowly into the living room. He didn't feel comfortable looking a gift horse in the mouth, but he mustered up the courage to ask, "Why, Mr. George?"

George walked over and took a seat in one of the Bernhart chairs, and gestured for Todd to sit down on the couch. With a look of sincerity, he said, "Well, every once in a while, I like to help make dreams come true for people that I care for. This time I chose you."

Todd shook his head in disbelief and said, "No, I cannot accept this from you. I can't do it. For a moment, I got caught up, enraptured with the idea of all this belonging to me—this being my new life. But then I realized, no, this can't be true." He then asked, "What did I do to deserve this?"

Choosing not to entertain Todd's flabbergasted nature, George pulled out papers from his jacket pocket. He affirmed Todd and said, "You absolutely can have this kind of life, and I am giving it to you—right now. This house is sitting on twenty acres of land, and here is information from a bank account that has $5.5 million in it, and it is all in your name. Oh, and you do not have to worry about any bills because I switched everything from manual to automatic billing.

Todd's jaw dropped.

"You put $5.5 million in a bank account just for me? Unreal. I can't believe it! How and when did you have time or even manage to do all of this in five days?"

"I didn't do it alone," said George, "About twenty-five other people helped make it happen."

Tears rolling down his face, Todd rocked back and forth, unable to sit still.

"But why me?"

George reminded Todd. "And I quote: *I don't want to be found dead in a gutter.*"

Todd wiped his eyes and asked if he could share his final wish. George was all ears and listened intently.

"Mr. George, when God calls me home, can you dress me in a burgundy suit and a beige shirt and lay me in a dark brown casket?"

"Your wish is my command, my friend. I promise."

For the next five months, two times a week, George visited Todd at the beautiful, tiny house and spent a couple of hours with him. Every time he went, however, he noticed a decline in his friend's health and that he seemed to be inching closer to his demise.

On his next and what would be their final visit together, he noticed that Todd wasn't looking good at all and was having trouble breathing. Asking him one last time if he wanted to go to the hospital, unsurprisingly, Todd said no. When George walked into the kitchen to grab a cold bottle of water from the refrigerator, he noticed that it was still full of food. Todd hadn't eaten in days.

George walked back into the living room and asked Todd if he thought he could hold down a couple of sips of tomato soup. Sitting still on the couch and staring directly at the television, Todd didn't reply. George waved Todd off and walked back into the kitchen to make a stiff one and make a couple of business calls. When he walked back into the living room this time, he sat in the opposite seat of Todd, picked up the remote, and changed the channel. He knew that would put the fire under Todd's britches and make him fuss at him for interrupting his favorite game show, Family Feud. Todd didn't budge, sitting still in the same position with the same look on his face.

George turned off the TV and sat there for a minute before whispering, "Hey, Todd, are you still with me?"

Realizing his friend was dead, George became emotionally overwhelmed, which was unexpected. He thought about Todd's end-of-life wishes and committed to honoring them.

Before driving Todd's body about a third of a mile down the road from the tiny house, deep in the woods, George dressed him in a burgundy suit and beige tie as requested. Upon arriving at the burial plot he dug a few months prior, he laid his friend to rest in a beautiful, brown casket. Leaning over it, he viewed Todd for the last time and noticed that he looked peaceful and fulfilled. George gathered his thoughts and silently eulogized him before pushing the casket over into the hole.

CHAPTER 19

6:18 am

After finally falling asleep, George woke up to the sound of Bruiser's barking. When he looked out the window, he saw a family of raccoons running through the junkyard. After yawning and stretching his stiff body, he decided to leave to find another hideout while it was still dark because it wasn't in his best interest to be there when the workers returned.

Peeking out of the fence, where he entered, he checked to see if the coast was clear. It wasn't. A police car drove by slowly, shining his bright spotlight. If he had left at that moment, he would have been caught red-handed. He had no choice but to wait a bit longer before his next attempt.

About ten minutes later, he peeked out the fence again, noticed that the coast was clear, and left. After walking a few blocks undetected, he saw a Goodwill drop-off box situated about fifty feet away. Searching the bin quickly, rummaging through every bag to find something else to change into, he was surprised but more frustrated not to find a single garment of clothing for men. Everything he pulled out of the bags was either for a woman or a child. He cringed at the last outfit he came across and tossed it to the side because it was ugly. Throwing a temper tantrum like a child, he started smacking his head with both hands, whining and grunting because he couldn't find anything suitable to wear. After sighing and grinding his teeth, he looked down at that disgusting outfit, snatched it up, evaluated it, and immediately became disappointed that it was an extra, extra-large, hot pink, metallic, one-piece jumpsuit. He grudgingly accepted that he had to do the unthinkable. Wear it.

While changing his clothes, every fiber within him caused him to cringe in disbelief. Knowing he had to cover his head, he put on a yellow cap designed for a woman to complete his look. Knowing he looked like a damn fool, he had no choice but to grin and bear it. Once finished, he picked up all the clothing, including the dirty, soiled clothes he was wearing, and placed everything back into the dropbox. To avoid looking suspicious to any patrolling cops, he walked casually up the street to appear as normal as possible.

Extremely hungry and thirsty, he knew he had to find food soon. When he arrived at the Gasser Up gas station, he approached a group of people and asked in a soft, timid voice, "Do any of you have spare change you can give me? I'm so hungry."

He avoided looking directly at their faces. Some people ignored him, and others looked at him like he was crazy. But, one woman said, "If you're that hungry, I'll buy you a meal."

George sighed with relief. "Please and thank you so much. I appreciate you!"

When she saw the sincerity on his face, she asked him, "What would you like to eat?"

"As they say, beggars can't be choosy, so I'll take whatever you'll buy me."

Nerves all over the place, George paced the parking lot while waiting for the lady to return with the food. As soon as she put the bag in his hand, he pulled the sausage breakfast sandwich out, ripped the wrapper off of it, and ate half of it in one bite, nearly choking as he swallowed.

The lady patted him on the back. "Please, sir, slow down before you choke yourself to death," while handing him a bottle of water.

A police car pulled up, looking at them both, and drove through the gas station, parking his car in a space close to where they were standing. George pretended not to see the cop and thanked the lady as he walked away.

"Excuse me, what is your name?" she asked.

George pretended like he couldn't hear her and kept walking. She ran up behind him and tapped him on the shoulder, startling him. He gasped and clutched his chest.

"My bad," she said, "I didn't mean to frighten you."

"I'm fine."

"What is your name?" she asked again.

"Georgie."

"Hi, Georgie! My name is Selena. I volunteer over on Douglas Street, where the homeless shelter is. I've never seen you over here before."

Pretending to cry, George said, "I haven't been out here that long."

"You'll be okay. Is it alright if I share some street survival tips with you?"

"Sure, please do!"

Ushering him back to the gas station, she explained everything he needed to know about living on the streets. "You see, normally, I would not do this, but you're so far away from the homeless shelters."

Selena went into her pockets and pulled out two bus tickets. Handing him one at a time, she explained, "Okay, so this ticket expires tonight at 7:20 p.m. It goes from here and will take you as far as downtown."

Handing him the second one, she explained further, "You can use this one tomorrow from downtown, and it will take you to any other part of the city you wish to go—one way." She then handed him a five-dollar bill.

"You just don't know how much your help means to me. Thank you so much," exclaimed George.

Feeling very uncomfortable, he leaned in and gave Selena a friendly hug.

"Okay, I gotta go now," Selena said, "Take care of yourself, Georgie."

"I will!" he replied as she was walking away. Suddenly, he yelled out to her, "Hey, Selena, what is the name of that company you volunteer for?"

"There is no particular company. I volunteer here, there, and everywhere in my spare time."

"Well, once I get on my feet, I would like to give to your spare time. How would I go about making a donation?" Selena giggled and walked away.

"Wait, Selena, what time is it?"

She didn't hear him, but a man riding a bike did. He looked at his watch and yelled out, "6:18 a.m."

George noticed that the area was heavily equipped with surveillance cameras and police patrol cars but took his chances and hopped onto the bus loaded with commuters. The bus was so full he had no choice but to stand and hold onto the rail. A lady, who was sitting in front of him, made him feel uneasy, staring at him the whole time as if she was trying to figure out a riddle. *Is it or is it not him?* He got off three blocks from his destination, and as the bus pulled away, the lady turned all the way around, gazing at him until he was out of sight.

Instead of going to the homeless shelter, George decided to hang out under the bridge on Douglas Street, where many homeless people live together. Selena told him that some people would rather live on the street than in shelters because they do not want people telling them what to do, how to do it, when to shower, and when to turn the lights off—and they don't like curfews. He encountered two other homeless guys when attempting to take the path that would lead him under the bridge.

One of them hocked and spit to his left side before asking, "Where do you think you're going?"

"Under the bridge with everyone else," George replied.

"What makes you think you're welcome to go down there?" asked the other homeless guy.

George took a couple of steps back and replied, "Well, Selena said..."

"Say no more. The mention of Selena's name gives you a free pass. Go right ahead. By the way, they call me Gatekeeper, and this is my friend Sidekick."

George shook their hands and introduced himself. "I'm Georgie."

A woman walked past them, heading under the bridge. She noticed that Sidekick was talking to a homeless guy she had never seen before. She conveniently walked over to them and introduced herself.

"Hi, my name is Clara. What is your name."

Sidekick answered for George and said, "Clara, this is Georgie! She is new around the area. Do you want to escort her down to our quarters and show her the ropes?"

As soon as she opened her mouth to speak, it stunned George because she sounded like the young woman from the coffee shop where he had first heard about the *BoJack Beer Distribution Company*.

Clara noticed that George was in deep thought and tapped him on the shoulder. "I know this must be a change for you," she said. He nodded yes.

"We are a close-knit family down here, and we look out for one another," she explained.

As they walked past the others, Clara introduced George to the rest of the group.

"Hey everyone, welcome Georgie to the family. She is new to the area. Please make her feel welcome and as comfortable as possible."

Simultaneously, everyone said, "Welcome!"

Introducing everyone by their first names, Clara pointed, "Over here is Tony and his girlfriend Sala. Over there is Rena, Jason, Eric, Carol, Brent, Stacy, Kristi, and Lori. A few other friends left earlier this morning to grab breakfast at the homeless shelter. They should be back shortly. If you ever want to stop by there, you can eat for free. Just let me know when you want to go. Oh, and there are two rules you MUST ABIDE by if you want to hang and camp out here."

"And those two rules are?" asked George.

"Do not touch anyone's possessions without asking, and you must show respect to everyone! That goes for everyone here."

Smiling, George said, "I can do that."

She then showed him her space under the bridge and said he could hang out there, offering him a seat on her queen-size mattress and box spring covered with a pretty red blanket and a few pillows.

"It's okay, Georgie. Kick your shoes off and relax!"

He hesitated before lying down. While listening to Clara engage in conversation with everyone else, George's mind drifted off to the time he was standing at the counter in the coffee shop near the college he attended.

"Can I take your order, sir?" asked the cashier.

"Yes, I would like a green tea frappe, no whip, no classic, add coconut milk," replied George.

She repeated his order before telling him the cost. "That'll be six dollars and thirty-four cents, sir."

After handing her a ten-dollar bill, she gave him his change. "Name for your order, please?"

"Bojack!"

"Bojack? I know that name!"

George blushed. "I come here often."

"No. I know it from somewhere else. Give me a minute!"

George stepped to the side so she could take the next person's order. After grabbing a seat at an empty table, he took a few sips of his drink and then pulled out his laptop and schoolwork to study. Several minutes later, the cashier rushed over to his table with a big smile on her face. George smiled back.

"Do you remember now?"

"Yes, my cousin works for the *Bojack Beer Distribution Company* in Indy. A few years back, I went to the company picnic. Have you ever heard of that company?"

"No, I have not."

"You should Google it! The owner, Mr. Bojack, is an awesome guy. He treats his employees very well."

"What is the owner's name again?"

"Mr. George Bojack," she repeated.

George felt like his soul had left his body. He needed a moment to process what the cashier had just told him, so he asked her if she could keep an eye on his stuff while he went to use the restroom. All kinds of thoughts rambled through his mind.

Could he be my father? If he is, why would my mother have kept me away from him? Maybe she was trying to protect me? Or, perhaps she was being cruel because of how he must have treated her.

George calmed his racing mind and decided not to jump to any conclusions. Grabbing a few paper towels and turning on the faucet to wet them, he wiped his face and left the restroom. While packing up his belongings, he thanked the cashier and proceeded to leave. He wanted to go back to his dorm room to research the *BoJack Beer Distribution Company* in private.

Before he could make it out of the coffee shop, the cashier stopped him. "Excuse me, sir! I just talked to my cousin in Indianapolis. She said that the next company picnic is in two weeks. Maybe you should check it out?"

"Maybe I will. Thanks."

George left in a hurry.

CHAPTER 20

A Bit Shocked

Before entering the picnic grounds, all the employees and their guests checked in at the registration desk to receive a name badge. When George stepped up to the desk, the receptionist didn't look up at him before asking for his name because she was too busy shuffling through paperwork.

"Your name, please?"

He hesitated. After receiving no response, she finally looked up at him. He then noticed the name on her badge and introduced himself.

"Hey Daphne, my name is George! George Bojack!"

Daphne sucked her teeth, and in a scolding manner, she said, "Look, sir! You're holding up my line. Other people are standing behind you, waiting to check in. Now, give me your correct name—please."

George quickly pulled his wallet out of his pocket, took out his license, and handed it to her.

With a perplexing look on her face, Daphne smiled. "My apologies, I thought you were kidding around. Your name really is George Bojack."

"Yeah, Daphne, my name is George Bojack."

After writing his name on a badge and handing it to him, she gave him the go-ahead to enter the picnic. A few other employees standing in line couldn't help but hear the exchange between George and Daphne. Wondering if he was their boss' son, word began to spread about George like wildfire.

When the news reached Catrina, she saw a young man walking around who indeed looked like Mr. Bojack. Thinking to herself, she said, *Unless Mr. Bojack himself had a facelift, then this man I am looking at does look like a younger version of my boss.*

She grabbed her phone and called him.

"Hello? Hello, Mr. Bojack?"

"Hello, Catrina."

"Sir, have you made it to the park yet?"

"We're pulling up right now as we speak. Is everything okay?

"I think so, but I'm not sure. I'll meet you at the front gate to explain."

Feeling as if all eyes were on him, George decides to leave the picnic. He could no longer take the pressure. As he proceeded to exit the park, he didn't get very far before hearing someone yell, "He's right there; he's leaving."

George noticed Daphne pointing at him. He then saw Catrina and a man resembling Mr. Bojack walking briskly towards him.

To get his attention, Catrina called out, "Hey, young man, hold on for a second! I want to introduce you to someone," while waiting for her boss to catch up to them.

Catching her breath, she said, "Alright, George Bojack, meet Mr. George Bojack!"

Mr. Bojack looked at George's face and saw a spitting image of himself as a young man. As his heart began to palpitate, he inhaled deeply and then doubled forward, grabbing his chest.

Catrina screamed, "Mr. Bojack!" before shouting, "Devin, catch him!"

Catrina looked around and quickly grabbed the nearest lawn chair.

"Devin, where is his portable oxygen tank?" she asked frantically.

"It's in the car because he refused to bring it, let alone carry it!"

"You know better, Mr. Bojack. Devin, will you go and get it, please?"

After picking up a few sheets of paper from the registration table, she started fanning her boss. Stunned at Mr. Bojack's reaction to seeing him, George became drawn to what was happening at the moment. At the same time, he became concerned. If Mr. Bojack was indeed his father, George didn't want anything to happen to him. After many years of yearning to someday meet the man who helped bring him into the world, he didn't want the opportunity that came out of nowhere to slip away. The moment felt surreal.

After Devin rushed to get the oxygen tank, he pushed through the curious crowd on his way back.

"Excuse me! Excuse me! I am coming through, people. Coming through!" he shouted.

Catrina couldn't see Devin but could hear him.

"Everyone, step back so that Mr. Bojack can breathe. Please, go and enjoy the picnic! We will take care of him. He's going to be just fine," advised Catrina.

After Devin sat the tank down, Catrina put the nasal cannula on Mr. Bojack. She gazed at him with frustration before mildly scolding him. "Now, you know you're supposed to keep this with you at all times, right, sir?"

After a few minutes of receiving oxygen, Mr. Bojack still couldn't catch his breath and struggled to breathe.

"Devin, please call 911!" instructed Catrina.

Mr. Bojack shook his head. "No, Catrina, no hospital! Just give me a few moments. I, I-I, I'm just a bit shocked, okay," while trying to catch his breath and rubbing his chest.

Despite his refusal to go to the hospital, Catrina made an executive decision for him to go anyway. Before the EMT could load him into the back of the ambulance, she asked him if he wanted her to call his wife, Bianca.

Looking over at George, he answered, "Yes, please do. And young man, will you accompany us to the hospital?"

George tried his best to hold back his tears. "Yes, sure, it would be my pleasure."

As the ambulance pulled off, the crowd dispersed and went back to enjoying the picnic.

After arriving at the emergency room and receiving intense treatment for nearly two hours, a nurse yelled out, "Visitors for Mr. Bojack?"

George and Catrina immediately walked across the waiting room to speak with the nurse to receive an update.

"How's he doing?" asked Catrina.

"He is stable, but the doctor wants him to stay overnight to undergo further observation. And by the way, he keeps asking to see you, young man. You're George, right?"

George grinned and shook his head, indicating his happiness to receive the good news. "Yes, I'm George."

"Okay, you can go back now, but try not to get him too excited. Head over to room seven," the nurse directed.

Leading the way, Catrina stopped herself. "It seems you guys might have a lot to discuss." Go on in, and I'll check in with you two shortly." George agreed.

The last time George visited a hospital was when his mother died. Standing in the doorway of Mr. Bojack's room, he gained his composure before entering. When Mr. Bojack opened his eyes and saw George standing there, he immediately grabbed at his face to remove the nasal cannula.

"Should you be taking that off, sir?" asked George.

Admitting that he shouldn't, grudgingly, he put the device back on his face and began scratching his head.

"I have so many questions to ask you, young man."

"Can you ask them later? The nurse advised that you not get too excited. It would be best if you relaxed for the time being. I'm sure we will have an opportunity to talk later."

"Okay, I must ask you this one question now," asserted Mr. Bojack.

George nodded, "Go ahead, sir."

"What is your mother's name?"

"Deborah Olsen Bojack."

Mr. Bojack quickly sat up and asked, "Did you say Deborah?!" gasping and internalizing the possibility that his flesh and blood could be sitting right beside him. His reaction sent his blood soaring and his heart rate racing, setting off the monitor's alarm. Hustling into the room, the nurse asked, "Mr. Bojack, are you okay? how do you feel?"

"I feel fine!"

"Well, that's not what the monitor reflects. Young man, maybe we need to let Mr. Bojack get some rest."

George stood up. "Sure, I agree. As I said before, we can talk later when you're feeling better."

Mr. Bojack gave him a stern look. "No! I want you to stay."

George obediently sat back down. The nurse looked over at the monitor again and saw that Mr. Bojack's vitals were back to normal levels. She then shrugged her shoulders and left the room.

Mr. Bojack laid back on his bed and got comfortable. "I know I'm not supposed to ask any more questions right now, but how is your mother?"

Looking down at the floor and hesitating, George decided to respond. "She died when I was eight years old."

Upon hearing this news, a flood of memories bombarded Mr. Bojacks's mind, overwhelming him to the point he became speechless for a few moments. He couldn't help but feel stunned. A single tear fell down his cheek, but George couldn't see it because of where he was sitting. The news concerning Deborah's death hit Mr. Bojack hard.

"Who took care of you all this time?"

"I had no known family and was placed in foster care."

"How did they treat you?"

"My adopted sister's name is Rachel. She treated me well, and she let me keep my last name."

Dr. Pence knocked on the door before entering. He shook both their hands and began to share the assessment he received from the nurse. "Mr. Bojack, you were a little overwhelmed today, and it was a bit too much for your heart." He then turned to George and asked him to leave so that he could examine his patient.

"This will not take long, so don't go too far," instructed Mr. Bojack.

"Oh, I won't, sir."

George stood in the hallway sorting through his emotions, which were all over the place. He thought to himself, *If only I had researched the Bojack name sooner.*

After the doctor completed his exam, Mr. Bojack asked him if he could order a DNA test. The doctor asked, "For what purpose?"

"Well, to be honest with you, I want to know if the young man standing on the other side of that door is my biological son?"

"Sure, no problem. Does he consent to take the test?"

"I'm not sure, but we are about to find out. Can you ask George to come back into the room, please?"

Dr. Pence opened the door and gestured for George to come back in.

"Young man?"

George interrupted. "My name is George."

"Okay, George. Mr. Bojack is requesting to have a DNA test for the two of you today. Do you have any objections?"

George's face became visibly flushed. "No, no. What do I need to do?"

"First, please have a seat before you hit the floor." Dr. Pence continued. "As for you, Mr. Bojack, after we get the results, I think we need to keep you here for another couple of days for further observation. Your vitals have fluctuated quite a bit, and we want them to stabilize." The doctor left.

The room was silent because both men were in their thoughts. Anyone could hear a pin drop. A few minutes later, a nurse entered the room and caught wind of the silence. She interrupted it when she informed them she was there to draw blood for their DNA tests.

"Now, Mr. Bojack, normally it takes two to three days to receive test results, but the doctor ordered your results STAT, which means you'll receive them in approximately four hours or less."

Mr. Bojack asked George, "Do you have time to wait? And by the way, I am sorry if I blindsided you with this request."

George sighed, "Yes, yes, I need to know! No, I want to know!"

"Well, I hope you get the results you're looking for!" replied the nurse.

George's leg shook uncontrollably.

"Mr. Bojack?" Catrina asked while knocking on the door and peeking into the room, "May I come in, sir?"

"Yes, Catrina, come on in so long as you don't start fussing," smiling when she entered the room.

"No, no more fussing from me today, sir."

Looking behind her, Mr. Bojack wondered where Bianca was. "Catrina, is Bianca here?"

"No, she's not here."

Disappointment consumed Mr. Bojack's face. "Is she coming?"

"Don't worry, sir. I texted her earlier. Unfortunately, I didn't hear back from her, but maybe she'll arrive at any moment. Would you like for me to go over to the house and check on her?"

"No. What I would like for you to do is head back over to the park and make sure everyone is having a good time!"

"Okay. Given that I know you're in good hands, I have no problem leaving you here and heading back to the park. I'm sure that many people will bombard me with questions I won't be able to answer once I arrive.

CHAPTER 21

It's A Boy

Later that evening, the nurse returned with an envelope and handed it to Mr. Bojack. Looking visibly nervous, "Is this what I think it is?" he asked.

"Yes. I'll leave you two alone," the nurse replied.

Mr. Bojack gave the envelope to George and told him to read it. Pausing for a moment, he slowly opened it. As he read the results, a tear rolled down his cheek.

He looked up at his father and said, "I never thought this day would ever come. Is it okay if I call you dad?"

With excitement, Mr. Bojack grabbed the paper. After reading the results himself, he tossed it in the air and yelled out, "It's a boy, 99. 9%! I have a son!"

He then cried like a baby. Shouting from the top of his voice, hoping Deborah could hear him from heaven, "Thank you, Deborah, thank you for not listening to me. You blessed me with a son! Oh my goodness, I have a son!" he exclaimed.

The nurse rushed back into the room because she heard Mr. Bojack yelling at the top of his lungs, and then she witnessed him fall off of the bed. Rushing over to help him up off the floor, he jumped up as if nothing was ever wrong with him and threw his hands in the air.

He yelled out again, "I have a son, I have a son!" grabbing the nurse's face and kissing her on the forehead.

She rejoiced in his excitement but replied, "Wonderful, Mr. Bojack. I'm happy for you, but you need to calm down. We don't need another health scare.

Not seeming to care one bit about what the nurse was saying to him, he danced and hopped around the room. He yelled out once again, "Deborah, we have a son!"

"Again, congratulations, sir! If you do not settle down, you are bound to have a heart attack." While pointing at the monitor, she asked, "Do you see your heart rate? It's climbing rapidly."

"I would rather look at my son," he replied.

He saw George sitting on the edge of the bed with his hands locked and his head down. Mr. Bojack calmed down, sat next to his son, and put his arm around his shoulder. The nurse quietly left the room.

In an angry voice, George whispered, "Why would she do this? Why would she keep me from you?"

"I can explain, son. She was protecting you from me."

"What reason would she need to protect me from you?"

Mr. Bojack realized that if he wanted to keep his son in his life, he had to tell the truth about what happened. Feeling embarrassed, he started to squirm in his seat. As he mustered up the courage to explain, his head fell into his chest.

"The morning your mother told me she was pregnant, I drove her down to a back-alley abortion clinic."

George stood up and walked over to look out the window.

"After I told her we both needed to think about what we would lose if she had a baby and how hard our struggles would be, she told me that she absolutely agreed. When she kissed me on the cheek and got out of the car, she asked me to wait for her and that she would return after undergoing the procedure. When she entered the building, I witnessed her holding her stomach tightly. I truly thought I convinced her to go through with having an abortion. After waiting for several hours, I checked in with the receptionist to see how long she would be. I learned that your mother checked in and quickly exited out the back door. She never came back, George. Honestly, that was the last time I saw her. I pushed for the abortion because we both had plans to go to college, and we both received full academic scholarships. Here's the bottom line, son. I chose college, and she chose you." Mr. Bojack's eyes welled up with tears. "But I'm glad to know that she made up her mind and did what she thought was best."

"Dad, did you ever try to find her?"

"Yes, I did. After I graduated, common sense kicked in. I searched for Deborah Olsen, not knowing that she had changed her name to Bojack. I figured she had gotten married and sailed off into the sunset."

At this point, George had bitten the inside of his jaw. "No. She never got married, and I do not recall her dating anyone. Do I have other siblings?"

"No, I do not have any other children. You see, I did a terrible thing to myself. I got a vasectomy thinking it would solve that problem during my college days. But the meaning of real-life set in when I went to have the procedure reversed. The doctor who performed the surgery botched it, and now I can never biologically father any more children. It devastated me because I wanted so badly to have babies of my own."

The nurse knocked on the door lightly and poked her head into the room. Jokingly, she asked if it was safe to enter. Mr. Bojack gestured with his hand that it was.

"I know that you two are in the middle of an emotional moment, but my shift is ending. Before I leave, I need to check your vitals and document them one last time."

Once finished, she looked at both men and smiled. "Mr. Bojack, try to contain your happiness, okay."

"I'll try, but it won't be easy."

"Well, I hope you guys have a peaceful and restful night. See you tomorrow, Mr. Bojack. Goodbye!"

He and George looked at her and said, simultaneously, "You should never say *goodbye!*"

Surprisingly, they looked at each other, not expecting the other to blurt out the exact phrase. George gave the nurse an explanation.

"When I was a little boy, my mother told me never to say goodbye to anyone but rather say *see you later* because *goodbye* could mean final, over, never again. *See you later* gives a person hope that they might see someone again in the future."

Mr. Bojack concurred, "Yup, that's my boy!"

The nurse chuckled and replied, "Okay, guys, I'll see you later."

Mr. Bojack immediately focused his attention on George. "Son, can I get a good look at you for a moment. I want to admire my child, who I didn't know existed all these years."

After studying his face and strikingly similar features, he then asked, "Son, will you please forgive me for missing out on all your firsts?"

George could see the sadness that attempted to invade his father's happiness, so he tried to humor him. "My first word was probably *da-da-da*, and I'm sure my first step looked something like this."

He stood up and walked like an infant taking its first steps. After stumbling over his feet and losing his balance, Mr. Bojack held out his hands to his son as if he was guiding and helping his baby to stay upright.

"I got you, my boy!"

"I believe you! Dad, would you like to hear about my first fishing trip?"

"I would love to, son!"

"Okay. When I was six years old, mom took me to a fishing tournament that her job was hosting. We went over to the reservoir a few times before the actual contest, and that is where she taught me how to fish. After putting the bait on my hook, I tossed my pole out over the water just like she told me. I followed her instructions like a big boy.

"Noooo, you didn't, son."

"Yes, I did, dad! I let go and tossed the whole fishing pole into the water!" They both burst out with laughter.

George told his father about all the first times he could remember, and Mr. Bojack shared most of his life memories with his son. Before long, they noticed it was past midnight. Looking at the time, George yawned and told his dad that he had to get going."

"Please stay, son," Mr. Bojack begged, "I don't want to share you with the world right now."

The sound of those words comforted George's soul. "Sure, Dad, I understand. I'll stay."

Mr. Bojack pushed the nurse's call button to request extra blankets and a pillow.

CHAPTER 22

Damn, Dad!

The following morning, Mr. Bojack told Dr. Pence he felt well enough to go home. The doctor agreed. "You are free to go, only if you promise not to get overly excited. Your CHF is nothing to mess around with."

"His CHF?" asked George.

The doctor asked Mr. Bojack if he had permission to share his personal health information with George.

"By all means, go ahead; he's my son!" Mr. Bojack said proudly.

Dr. Pence explained to George, "He has a systolic failure, which means his heart is failing on the left side, causing the left ventricle to lose the ability to function normally. In simpler terms, his heart is not strong enough to push a significant amount of blood into circulation. I'm sad to say this, but he's on the last of four stages. I advise you and the family to prepare for the worst."

"This is why I would love for you to relocate to Indianapolis and take over the business before I die," Mr. Bojacked explained to George.

As Bianca, Mr. Bojack's wife, walked into the room, she overheard him say the word *die*. "So, finally, the truth is revealed. Are you dying? And how quickly is this supposed to happen?" she asked with a heartless and nasty attitude.

Her question disgusted Doctor Pence, causing him to leave the room immediately.

She looked at George and purred, "Hey, handsome, who are you?"

Mr. Bojack spoke up boastfully. "Hey there, slow your roll! You're purring at my handsome son."

"Son? He shows up out of nowhere, tells you he's your son, and you're just going to believe him?"

Abruptly interrupting her line of questioning, George spoke up. "Dad, I'm going to head down to the cafeteria for breakfast, but before I go, allow me to introduce myself properly."

George extended his hand to Bianca. "My name is George Bojack, Jr. It's my pleasure to meet you."

With a skeptical look on her face, Bianca asked, "Really? Your name is George?"

"Yes, it is."

Placing her hands on her hips, she continued to question him. "So, I guess you're going to play this out to the fullest? Name change and all, right?"

George looked at his father, shrugged his shoulders, and walked out of the room.

When the door closed, Bianca asked her husband, "So, when did you find out you had a son?"

"To my surprise, yesterday!"

"Yesterday? To be such an intelligent man, you sure are gullible. Some random dude walks into your hospital room and tells you he's your son, and you believe him. I cry bullshit! How much money did he ask you for?"

Handing Bianca the results of the DNA test, he responded, "Not as much as you have."

"Just what in the hell is this? What does it mean? DNA test? Is this even real? Anyone can type up this crap!"

"Now, before you go assuming, yesterday I asked Dr. Pence to test us, and the results came back conclusively proving that he belongs to me by 99.99%."

Bianca couldn't believe what she was hearing and huffed and puffed before tossing the paper onto the bed and storming out of the room.

After leaving the cafeteria, George stepped outside of the hospital to get some fresh air. Baffled and concerned, he saw his father's wife in the arms of another man and stood there in disbelief, especially after witnessing her rant and rave to this man about how she has to share her husband's time and money with someone else. George wanted to make his presence known, so he walked over to her and her male friend.

"Hey, what should I call you? Mom?"

"BIANCA! You're too damn old to call me mom," she barked.

"And your name is, sir?" he asked the man.

Giving him the evil eye, Bianca shouted, "It's none of your damn business what his name is!"

She grabbed the man's hand and said in the most threatening and nastiest voice George had ever heard, "If you say anything to your father about this, it will probably stop him from breathing. See you later, you bastard!"

With all of his heart, George wanted her to say *goodbye* so bad.

After George relocated to Indianapolis, his father taught him how to run the beer distribution business. Bianca didn't like it one bit that her husband's son encroached into her territory. The more she realized how inseparable they had become, she stopped hanging out at night and tried to stay home more to appear to be a better wife. Her disingenuous efforts failed. Eventually, she was no longer welcome and excluded from attending family functions.

Seven months later, Bianca and George found themselves sitting in the office of Mr. Bojack's attorney, waiting to learn the details of his will. George was still mourning the loss of his father while Bianca sat back glowing, ready to receive her check and blow the joint.

When a female attorney entered the room, Bianca stated sternly, "I choose not to sit and listen to you babble on about this, that, and the other. Please give me what he left for me so I can get on with my business!"

The attorney extended her hand to George and introduced herself. "My name is Attorney Cora York, and our firm Sykes and Grier has been representing your father for more than ten years."

George reached across the table to shake her hand and then introduced himself. "Hello, Attorney York, my name is George Bojack, Jr."

Bianca did not like the sound of that and snapped. "Stop your damn lying! You know good and well that you're not a Junior!"

Shuffling through a stack of organized papers, the attorney pulled out a specific form. "Well, Mrs. Bojack, George is a Junior. Your husband added his son to his will six months ago with a name change. Rubbing it in, the attorney then said, "Nice to finally meet you, Mr. George, Jr."

"What a pleasure it is to meet you, ma'am."

The attorney looked at Bianca with a slight grin on her face and thought to herself, *put that in your pipe and smoke it*! Aloud, she said, "Now, I will begin to read the contents of the will."

Turning to George, she explained, "When you appeared in your father's life, you made him the happiest man in the world. It was his pleasure to leave you everything!"

George gasped, "Everything?" he asked.

Bianca stood up and leaned forward over the desk. "If he left everything to him, what did he leave for me?"

The attorney continued to speak directly to George, "The business, the house, the cars, all three bank accounts, all seven properties, and everything else that has his name on it. He left it all to you, George. I have the list here; we can discuss it when she leaves."

Bianca insisted, "I'm not leaving until you give me what he left for me."

The lawyer handed her an envelope with her name on it. Bianca ripped it open. "What the hell is this?"

"The reason you're not entitled to any of your husband's possessions is legally you're not his wife.

"Huh," Bianca responded.

"You failed to submit your paperwork to the court within thirty days after you two said *I do*. The purpose of submitting that document was to validate your marriage, and fortunately for Junior, you missed that deadline. Mr. Bojack reminded you on several occasions to take care of this matter, and you ignored him every time. On day thirty-one, my office received this envelope providing specific instructions on how to carry out his wishes and to give you these pictures," Attorney York explained.

With no remorse, the attorney tossed the envelope and pictures onto the desk and leaned back into her chair. "Any more questions, Mrs. Bojack? Oh no, you're not Mrs. Bojack. What should I call you?"

George peeked over at the pictures and noticed that they were of Bianca and the man he saw her hugged up with at the hospital. He whispered to himself, "Damn, Dad, checkmate!"

CHAPTER 23

No, It Can't Be

George snapped back to reality when he heard a familiar voice talking to Clara. He realized it was Sharon, Todd's old girlfriend, who hung out with him near the *Bojack Beer Distribution Company*. He knew if she saw his face, she would blow his cover. Clara tapped his foot to get his attention; he seemed to be somewhat out of it.

"Miss Georgie, honey, it's almost lunchtime. Let's get ready. By the way, I want to introduce you to my bestie, Sharon,"

Pretending to be asleep, George shifted his body with his face still in his arm, "OK, let me wake up, first."

Sharon and Clara walked to the back of the bridge to hang out with everyone else. George saw this as the perfect moment to escape. He rolled off the mattress onto the ground, crawled across the entrance, and walked away without being noticed.

He asked a few homeless people who didn't recognize him to direct him to the bus terminal. Once he got there, he kept a low profile until after the lunch rush was over. He then jumped onto the E. Briteway bus line, knowing that the last stop would put him out three miles from the little house in the woods. After getting off the bus, he had no other choice but to walk the rest of the way.

About an hour and a half later, a calm came over him when he noticed that the little house was in eye's view. When he reached the house, he dropped to his knees and reached under the porch for a black tin box, where he kept a spare key. Upon entering the house, he checked the hiding place where he stashed $200,000, several prepaid phones, and keys for the black pickup truck with tinted windows in the garage. He had everything he needed.

George decided to take a long, hot shower. While showering, he thought about how he hadn't had much to eat in the last few days and how hungry he was. Recalling memories about everything that happened after Todd died, from clearing out the kitchen pantry to restocking everything and burning the couch that Todd died on in a bonfire, his emotions started to get to him. He quickly shook them off.

With a variety of options in mind—steak, chicken, fish and shrimp, lamb chops, and more—he decided on a simple choice to boil some authentic, hearty gourmet udon noodles. After enjoying dinner, he booted up his laptop and logged in to access a tracking app that would help him hunt and track down Devin and his once-beloved Pilar.

Pilar and Devin were on their way home from their new jobs but drove in separate cars. Instead of going straight home, which was only a few blocks away from her job, Pilar stopped by the drugstore to grab some Alka Seltzer and a few other items. She had not felt well for the last few days and thought she was coming down with the stomach flu. While walking to the back of the store, a pregnancy test caught her eye. She took a couple of steps back, looked at the box, and whispered to herself, "No, I can't be pregnant," before picking up the box and tossing it into her basket. When she arrived home, she didn't hesitate. She took the test, and instead of waiting around for the results, she jumped in the shower to kill some time.

After showering, she heard a noise on the other side of the bedroom door and rushed to put on her clothes. Devin had a bad habit of bringing company over without telling her. She grabbed the pregnancy test, and before she could leave the bedroom, George appeared in the doorway. For a moment, they stood in place and stared each other down.

George mumbled, "I told you never say *goodbye!*"

Fear came over Pilar, and she immediately tried to get away. George grabbed her around the neck and strangled her. She fought him with all her might. As she started to faint, she uttered the words, "I'm pregnant."

George removed his hands from her neck, and after letting her go, she fell and hit her head on the corner of the dresser. Blood splashed and spread everywhere. He then heard someone come into the house, calling out to Pilar. It was Devin.

"Bae, I'm home!" He started singing to himself as he took off his shoes. He yelled out again, "Bae, where you at?" He heard noises coming from the bedroom and called out to her again. "Bae?"

He became concerned and went to check on her because she wasn't responding. When he walked into their bedroom, he could not believe his eyes. Pilar was lying on the floor in a puddle of blood. "No, no!" he cried, "Baby, what happened?"

After hearing a loud thump outside his bedroom window, he looked out and saw his former boss running away. He ran back over to Pilar to try and wake her up. He didn't want to move her too much to avoid causing her any more pain than she might have been feeling. He brushed her hair out of her face and began to kiss her forehead, asking her to wake up.

"Talk to me, Pilar, talk to me. Please, baby, talk to me." After begging her, he screamed uncontrollably.

Derrick and Keisha, Devin and Pilar's friends, had just pulled into the driveway. As Derrick opened his car door, they heard Devin screaming at the top of his lungs and rushed up to the house and began knocking on the door.

Keisha yelled, "Hello, Pilar, Devin, it's us. What's going on in there?"

After hearing more screaming, Derrick used his body to push open the door. When they got inside, they realized that Devin was in his bedroom. Thinking that he might need some help, they ran into the bedroom and found Devin in despair and Pilar lying lifeless on the floor bleeding.

"Someone, please help her, please!" he begged.

Keisha sat down next to Devin and asked if he could give her some space. Immediately, she looked for Pilar's pulse and had difficulty finding one, and began performing CPR. Derrick called 911. After doing several rounds of CPR with no success, Derrick took over. When they switched places, Keisha found a white plastic stick stuck under Pilar's right hip, which looked like a pregnancy test. She pulled it out from under her and quickly put her hand over her mouth.

"Devin," Keisha said as she handed the positive pregnancy test over to him, "I'm so sorry!"

He pushed Derrick out of the way and grabbed Pilar, holding onto her tightly. "I'm sorry, baby, I'm sorry. Everything is going to be alright, okay baby!" he cried.

After they heard the sirens of the ambulance and police, Keisha went outside to meet with them.

George ran back to his truck, where he parked a block away. After driving off, he started beating his steering wheel so hard that he broke his pinky finger. "I'm sorry, precious baby; I didn't know you were in there!" he said emotionally.

Hearing sirens coming in his direction, he made a quick right turn and watched through his rearview mirror as they passed by. His pinky throbbed like hell, so he held it against his chest and drove with the opposite hand.

CHAPTER 24

Study of Bugs

I mmersed in deep thought about what just happened, George drove as far as he could until his truck ran out of gas. It stalled on Interstate 65 in the state of Tennessee in front of a Nashville exit. After contacting roadside service to bring him gas, he found a country radio station on his cell phone. To his surprise, he heard Reba say, "Good night to all the country music lovers within the sound of my voice. Sleep tight."

While waiting for roadside assistance to show up, he drifted off into another recollection dating back to his first year of attending college at Ball State University where met Reba.

Every Monday through Friday, at 1:00 pm, George would head over to the campus bookstore. On this particular day, when he approached the counter, Reba, the cashier, flashed a seductive smile at him and boldly said in her country twang, "Excuse me, sir. Why do you come in here, it seems like every day, to purchase one pencil for a buck fifty when you can buy an entire pack of five for $2.99?"

"It's now or never," George thought to himself. "My name is George Bojack. I'm a student here, and I live in

Waller Hall. I know this might seem a bit forward, but would it be okay if I take you to lunch one day? Or how about today, dinner on campus at the café?" he asked.

Reba recalled what her mama once told her.

When you find a man constantly sniffing around you, he has a motive, usually the "I want to court you" one.

As George blushed, she winked at him. "Well, now, look at you. You are beet red! And you have such a big handsome smile that I can count every one of your pearly whites. Mama said that you can always tell how a man takes care of himself when he opens his mouth," she said, carrying on, "Yes, I'll be more than delighted to go on a date with you."

After dinner, they went for a walk around the campus. Reba did all the talking, and George listened so that he'd be prepared for any quiz she might give him at the end of the date.

"I love Nashville. There is no other city like it. My most favorite place to visit is the Grand Ole Opry. It's beautiful. When I was ten years old, I auditioned for *The Grand Ole Opry Christmas Tale*, and I got the role three years in a row. Even though I was just a little ole twinkling star, I did my best to shine. When I turned fourteen, I mustered up enough courage to audition for a different role as a singing, wise girl. But the day before auditions, I was hanging out with Doddles and the General at my Granpap's farm in an old country town outside of Nashville."

"Doddles? General?" asked George.

"Doddles is my Granpap's favorite horse, and The General is his mean old rooster. He's meaner than me. He reminds me of a Pitbull. I dare you to walk up to the chicken coop and disturb his female chickens, and The General doesn't know who you are. You are going down! Anyway, Tiptoe..."

"Tiptoe?" George repeated.

"My Granpap's cat. She was chasing after a mouse, and I didn't see them coming. As they passed by me, I tripped over Tiptoe and broke my left arm," she explained. "George, have you ever eaten hot pickles and slaw?"

He shook his head no.

"Well, I love hot pickles. My Granpap jarred plenty of them up for me every year. The older they are, the better they taste," again, she carried on.

"Did I tell you who my favorite country singer is?"

Shaking his head. "No, but let me guess, Dolly?"

Reba shook her head. "No, but I love her!"

George cleared his throat. "Tammy?"

"Nope, but I love her too. You get one more guess, and if you don't get it right, I'm just gonna let the cat out of the bag."

George giggled.

"What about ... um ... um ... What's her name? Um, I think it's the same as yours." George tapped his forehead a few times. "I think I got it! Oh, shoot! And there it went. It slipped my mind," he said jokingly.

Reba rolled her eyes at him.

"Do you know that you're getting on my nerves right about now?" She punched him in his stomach and took off running.

George chased after her and yelled, "Come back here, Reba Mac!"

Reba stopped running and stomped her right foot. She said, "You joker! You knew all along!"

As they continued their walk, he asked her what her major was.

In the sweetest voice, she said, "I've been running off at the mouth the entire date. Ain't you tired of hearing my voice?"

Whispering in her ear, George said, "No."

She blushed and desperately wanted to hold his hand. Still, she could hear her Granpap repeatedly saying, *On your first, second, third, fourth, and fifth date, no kissing and holding hands, and what Granpap says goes.*

Reba finally answered. "My major is communication, and my minor is studying bugs."

"Bugs?" George asked while smiling.

"Yes, bugs. Entomology is the study of insects."

"And why are you interested in bugs?"

"Every time my Granpap saw a bug in the house, he did not hesitate to end the little critter's life. It would set my soul on fire, and I would get to fussing at him. One day I said, "Pap! Maybe it just wanted to come indoors out of the heat and cool off."

He fussed right back at me, "Maybe you have a point there, Reba. But, the uninvited critter forgot to pay at the door."

I stomped out of the house onto the back porch, where I found a tiny purple bug that I had never seen before. It was lying on its back, dead. I scooped it up in a jar and did some research to learn more about it and where it might have come from."

"Did you ever figure out what kind of bug it was?"

"Yes! The little booger turned out to be a Porcellio Scaber."

Shrugging his shoulders, George then asked, "And what kind of bug is that exactly?"

"Oh, it turned out to be a common rough woodlouse, a city bug. How it ended up far out in the country beats me."

"Maybe it was supposed to be bird food, and it got away."

"Yeah, that could be it because we did have a bird feeder outside our family room window. Now, let me tell you the reason it was purple. The poor tiny booger had iridovirus, which is a fatal infection and is prevalent in woodlice."

Reba stopped talking and looked over at George, who didn't seem enthused about listening to her talk about bugs.

"Well, you know what?! I've talked enough tonight to fill up an outhouse.."

George frowned at her expression about the outhouse.

"Oops, I didn't mean to brand your face with that look. I'm sure anyone would frown when associating outhouse with the *mouth*. I was only repeating something my Granpap would always say. Now, tell me something about you."

"Well, when my mother had me, she raised me by herself. I never knew or met my biological father even before she died. I also never got the chance to meet any of her family because she was an only child. And my grandparents died before I was born. Needless to say, I never knew my family while growing up and ended up in foster care."

George could sense that telling his story depleted sparks of joy from Reba's entire body.

"Reba, please don't be sad for me. I'm extremely grateful for being adopted by a remarkable young lady, my foster sister, Rachel. Let me not say the word *foster* because that detail is irrelevant. She is my sweet sister, and that is all. The first day I moved in with her, I asked her never to say *goodbye* to me, and please say *see you later*. She said that after reading my file, she would never let those awful words part her lips."

"Why is that word so ugly to you?"

Before answering her question, he stuffed his hands in his pockets and looked up to the sky. "*Goodbye* was the last word my mother spoke to me as she took her last breath."

"Oh me, oh my, you poor soul. I promise not to let that word slip out of my mouth!"

Standing directly in front of him, Reba reached for his hands and held onto them. She considered that the only way her Granpap would know if she held a man's hands on the first date is if she spilled the beans herself. She had no intention of doing that. It was getting late, and they had walked around most of the college campus before heading back to her dorm.

"My dear, sweet George, thank you for being such a kind gentleman and for giving me such a fun-filled evening."

He looked Reba in the eyes and said, "It was my pleasure hanging out and getting to know you."

She was about to say goodbye but said *goodnight* instead.

"Will I see you tomorrow?" asked George.

Reba blew a kiss at him, and he pretended to catch it and placed it on his cheek. She stood at the door of the dorms as George walked away.

"Tomorrow."

CHAPTER 25

Spicy Hot

For the next several weeks, Reba and George went on many dates. They went biking, roller skating (neither one could skate), to the movies, hung out at the pool, and more. They also became study buddies and endured many late-night sessions together to help each other prepare for pop quizzes and exams.

While getting dressed for her next date with George, Reba's roommate, Marjorie asked, "So, when do I get to meet your boy toy?"

"He's not a boy toy. He's a gentle gentleman," Reba replied.

"Gentleman? Really? So, you're saying he's never..."

"Nope. Not even a kiss. I think he's waiting for me to make the first move, and I believe it's time I showed him some affection on the hayride tonight."

"Oh, you nasty girl! What kind of affection?"

"Oh, just a smooch here and a smooch there."

"After all the smooching on the hayride, are you guys coming to the Truth or Dare Jam?"

"Truth or Dare Jam? Oh, heck yeah! Did they give out the location yet?"

"No, but as soon as I find out, I'll be sure to text you. But have fun on your date anyway. And don't do anything I would do."

"Oh, no! I won't! I have to get going, girl. I'll see you later."

As planned, Reba met George at the student center to walk to the hayride pickup location together. When George saw her, he lit up and complimented her look. "I love the country flair you got going on. You look very nice."

"Why, thank you, honey."

They thoroughly enjoyed themselves, and especially the scenic view that arrested their attention along the way, feeling as if they had no cares or worries in the world. As they were nearing the end of the ride, it surprised George when Reba grabbed his arm and placed it around her shoulders. Elated, he pulled her in close. She kissed his cheek and was about to go for the lips when she got a text and read it out loud.

"They have revealed the Truth or Dare Jam location. It's at the Walker Elks dorms. George, would you like to go with me and meet a few of my friends?"

Throwing up his hands, he said, "Sure. Why not..."

Before completing his response, Reba straddled her legs across his lap. While passionately serving him his first kiss, she briskly ran her fingers through his hair and then down his back and said in a captivating voice, "I done fell head over heels for you, boy."

George's body language gave her permission to move forward. After thrusting her hips back and forth a few times, the wagon came to a halt. The hayride was over.

Embarrassed and not thinking, George lifted her up from his lap and tossed her back onto the hay. After jumping off the wagon, he didn't hesitate to help her off, especially after the awkward moment they just had.

The driver thanked them both, then said, "I'd better hurry. I only have about thirty minutes to get my tractor gassed up for the next load of eight."

"Wasn't this ride supposed to be a load of eight as well?" asked Reba.

"Yes," replied the driver, "But your fella here...."

Reba caught George gesturing for the driver not to tell her what he had done.

"Okay, Mr. Fella, why all the secrecy?"

George started humming.

"I'm waiting for you to explain yourself, sir. Spit it out!" she demanded.

After receiving no response, she stepped up to him closely, pretending to be sad.

"So, we're starting our relationship with secrets?" After being told he was in a relationship, he immediately told on himself.

"The truth is I wanted to experience this hayride with you alone, so I purchased all eight of the tickets, kept two, and trashed the others."

Giggling, she responded, "Aww, that was so sweet of you!" She grabbed his hand, and they walked over to the Walker Elks Dorms.

Upon arriving at the Truth or Dare Jam, Reba warmly introduced George as her boyfriend. They indulged in complimentary refreshments and a couple of sweet teas and enjoyed themselves to the fullest until George noticed his former classmate and enemy, Tyrese, walk through the door. Reba noticed a sudden change in her man's demeanor.

"Honey, are you okay?"

Gritting his teeth, George tried his damndest not to allow his brewing anger to consume him.

Still visibly agitated, he replied, "Reba, I'm okay. Don't worry about me. You continue to enjoy yourself."

A few moments later, he walked over to a corner of the room and sat down in a chair. Making sure that his back was turned to no one, he kept his eyes on everyone— especially Tyrese.

A random guy commanded the crowd and yelled out, "Let the games begin!"

Showing their excitement, everyone began to cheer and clap.

The same dude yelled out, "And we must follow the rules. If you choose the truth, you must tell the truth and nothing but the truth! And if you choose the dare, you absolutely must follow through with the dare. Now, who's up first?"

Reba raised her hand. "I'll go first."

Another obnoxious roar swept throughout the room. And people who knew her chanted her name, "Reba, Reba, Reba, Reba…!"

The game host commanded everyone to quiet down so that he could hear her choice. "What do you say, truth or dare?" he asked.

Reba thought to herself. They *don't know too much about me, so I'm going to choose dare.* "Dare!" she shouted.

Unexpectedly, Tyrese stepped from behind the host and said, "Bro, let me do the honors of giving out the first dare."

Fright landed on George's face as he stood up. He then walked over to Reba and told her that it was time to go.

Peering at Reba, Tyrese asked, "What's the rush, George? What, you don't trust your girl?"

Someone from the crowd began to chant, "Take the dare, take the dare...," and then everyone else in the room joined in.

Reba took a step towards Tyrese and replied on her man's behalf, "Why wouldn't he trust me?"

Tyrese looked her up and down and pulled a pint of Hennessy out of his back pocket. "Okay, hot toddy, let's go then! I dare you to drink this in one gulp or tell your boy here *goodbye.*"

Torn about what to do, she thought to herself again.

Who do I love more at this moment, him or myself? If I choose to say goodbye, his feelings would be hurt, but only for a short time. I'll apologize and then kiss him on the tip of his nose and make it all better. Or, if

I choose not to say goodbye, I'll have to gulp down a pint of alcohol, which is insanely crazy. I'd be out of commission for days, and that is not a chance I'm willing to take with finals starting tomorrow.

Not knowing the repercussions of the words she was about to speak, Reba turned her back to George and whispered the word *goodbye*.

Tyrese shouted, "Yo, Reba! Why am I ear hustling to hear what you're saying? Speak up!"

The crowd agreed.

Turning back around, Reba faced George and mouthed the words, "Please understand," before belting out, "Goodbye, George."

After hearing her blurt out that forbidden word, his anger intensified. As he started to walk away, Reba tried to comfort him with a hug. Rejecting her, he shoved her away and headed for the exit. Tyrese made a mockery of the moment and directed everyone to chant *goodbye* to George.

"Goodbye, George! *Goodbye*, George!" they shouted.

George pushed his way through the crowd and left the party without Reba. She tried to catch up with him before he exited, but Tyrese ordered a couple of the guys to stand in front of the door. She became livid, and a vein popped out of her forehead. Gruffing, Reba threatened Tyrese's friends.

"If you do not move out of my way, both of your third legs will become dysfunctional for the rest of your lives!" They took her threat seriously and got out of her way. She didn't waste any time and ran straight to George's dorm, which was about five minutes away from Walker Elks.

When she arrived at George's dorm, she stood outside for about an hour, texting him and hoping he would answer. Eventually, she called it quits for the night and tried to contact him again the next day. She continued to look for him for weeks, to no avail. She never heard from him again.

This kind of hurt was different for George because he had come to care for and love Reba dearly. She was his first true love. Believing that if he allowed a significant amount of time to pass, he could dynamite any sense of emotional attachment and fall out of love with her—making it easier for him to take her life.

George's thoughts vanished when roadside assistance called to make him aware that a driver was en route and would arrive in less than ten minutes. He thought it was a perfect time to plan his attack, to pay Reba back for breaking her promise. After Googling her name and the address to the radio station where she worked, the information popped up on the first page. As he plugged the address into his GPS, a roadside assistance vehicle pulled up behind his truck. A short, stubby man with a ponytail and thick beard wearing a lime green reflective vest emerged from the car and opened the trunk to retrieve a five-gallon container of gas. After pouring just enough to ensure that George could make it to the nearest gas station to fill up his tank, the man asked him if he needed anything else.

Enthused about closing the final chapter with his first love, he said to the man, "No, I'm all set," before tipping him generously and speeding off.

George decided to rent a hotel room nearby for the night, which was a waste of money because he had difficulty sleeping. He debated with himself on exercising the quickest way to separate Reba's soul from her body. He thought,

> If I stab her quickly multiple times, she'll die right away. Naw, too bloody. If I choke her, it must be from the back because I would not have the courage to look her in the face. How about I plow her down as she crosses the street? Or, maybe I can find a desperate bum on the streets and pay him to kill her?

Finally, becoming restless at sunrise, George set his alarm to wake up at 4:00 pm, giving him plenty of time to rest. Around 5:00 pm, he posted outside the radio station until Reba got off work. When she pulled out of the parking lot, he followed her but made sure not to get too close. While driving, his thoughts took him back to when Reba told him how much she loved spicy pickles. Coincidentally, she stopped by the *Spicy Hot* food truck.

When she got out of her car, she walked over to the food truck and stood in line. Quite a few people stood in front of her. George parked his car several spaces away, got out, walked up, and stood directly behind her. When it was her turn, he overheard Reba order four spicy hots and a diet soda. The cashier repeated the order and told her that the total was $8.15. Searching her pockets for money to no avail, George reached around her and laid a twenty-dollar bill on the counter. He told the cashier to keep the change. Curious about who generously paid for her food, Reba slowly turned around and discovered it was George. Blinking her eyes and gasping uncontrollably, she jumped up into his arms and kissed him all over his face.

After every kiss, she repeated, "Forgive me! Please, please forgive me!"

Pretending to be equally excited, he held on to her tightly and thought about squeezing her to death. But then he spotted a boulder out of the corner of his left eye and imagined dropping her on her head, hitting it in the right place, and breaking her neck. But, fortunately for Reba, George's thoughts of harming her went dimmer with every kiss and sensation that arose as he caressed her body.

The cashier abruptly interrupted them. "Four hots and a diet soda," she called out.

Breathing heavily, Reba lowered herself to the ground and replied, "I believe that's my order," before swiftly grabbing the bag from the counter and jumping right back into George's arms.

"Please say you forgive me!" she begged.

He reached for her hand, walked her over to a picnic table, and offered her a seat.

After sharing her pickle with him, which he thought was delicious, she took a long gulp of her drink. "George, please pinch me so that I know that I'm not dreaming. You really are here with me sitting at this picnic table eating spicy pickles, right?"

Flashing a smile at her, he replied, "I promise you you're not dreaming."

With a serious look on her face, she explained, "I came looking for you after you stormed out of that party. For days, I followed your routine, and after trying to find you for quite some time, I gave up when I realized you didn't want to be found."

"I figured that's what you would do, so I changed some things around," George replied.

The talk of that night once more detonated thoughts of how he could eliminate her.

After taking another sip of her drink, Reba said, "George, if you're not going to accept my apology, then why did you come looking for me?"

A few of her fans walked by and noticed her.

"Hey, look, guys! It's Radio Reba!" one fan shouted.

She waved at them and said, "Thanks for listening, guys! I appreciate the love."

To play it safe, George pretended to tie his shoe so that none of her fans would notice him. He sat up and answered her question.

"I didn't come looking for you. I was headed south on highway 65 and remembered how you painted this city to be so beautiful. So, on a whim, I took the Nashville exit and drove around until I became hungry. I spotted the pickle truck and figured I'd stop by and try one. And there you stood in front of me."

"Wow! Fate—it must be fate," Reba exclaimed. "Oh my, I can't wait until you meet GG. She's going to love you."

Looking at the time, she realized she was running fifteen minutes late. "Oh my goodness, I have got to go. George, if I give you my address, will you meet me out at the farm?"

George grinned. "Sure."

She quickly wrote down the address and hurried to her car. While pulling off, she yelled back at George, "See you later."

CHAPTER 26

My Name Is GG

George was sitting in his truck outside of Reba's house when she arrived. After she got out of the car, he heard another car door shut but didn't see anyone. To his surprise, a little girl with strawberry blonde hair came walking in front of the car. She looked to be about five years old. In her tiny, twangy voice, she greeted George.

"Hello. My name is GG."

"GG is her nickname. George Gena is her given name," Reba explained.

Studying Reba's face, George repeated, "George Gena?"

"Yes, sir, my name is George Gena. What's your name?"

"Oh, my name is George."

Surprised, GG remarked, "Mommy, his name is almost like mine."

Changing the subject, Reba handed GG the house key and told her to go inside, run herself some bathwater, and get ready for dinner and movie night. George became smitten with GG when she said, "Yes, ma'am," following her mother's instructions without talking back.

"Come on, George, let's go into the house. I'll explain everything."

He sat at the kitchen table while she went to check on GG. When Reba returned, George asked, "Does GG really run her own bathwater and bathe herself?"

"Yes, she does."

"But she's only five!"

"And, at the age of five, she's capable of doing much more than running herself a tub of water."

"I can imagine that her dad is a proud father."

"No, he doesn't even know that she exists."

"Excuse me?"

"Well, here's the thing. Two hundred and forty-one days after you disappeared on me, I went out on a blind date with a jerk named Conrad. He was a student at the college, too. After having a couple of drinks, I believe he slipped me a mickey in one of them because I woke up in a hotel room the following morning alone and naked as a jaybird with a hangover. Wrapping myself up with a sheet, I got out of the bed and looked for my clothes. I couldn't find them, which was extremely odd. I then looked for my cellphone to call the police. I couldn't find it either. I saw a telephone on the nightstand by the bed, and when I tried to dial out, the phone was dead. I discovered that the phone cord was ripped out of the wall.

I felt like I was trapped in a box after realizing the bastard had taken off with all my stuff. I was angry and felt violated, and I thought about how I could allow this to happen to me. Not knowing what to do or how to help myself, I sat on the bed and cried, for how long I don't know. I calmed down and waited patiently. Finally, a lady from housekeeping showed up to clean the room. When I opened the door, she saw that I was in distress and asked me what was wrong. I didn't explain and asked her to call the police. When the police arrived, I told them what had happened. When the ambulance arrived, they took me to the hospital to receive an examination. After a doctor concluded that someone raped me, she gave me a molotov cocktail of medication to help prevent me from contracting any diseases.

Later that day, the police went and picked up Conrad and took him to the police station to question him. When asked if he put something in my drink and then took me to a hotel room, he swore up and down that he didn't know how I ended up there. He claimed that he dropped me off at my dorm and hadn't seen me since and that he had an alibi. His frat brother vouched for him and told the police that he had arrived home just before midnight. Long story short, the police didn't have enough evidence to charge him with a crime, so he got away with what he did to me. I was in total disbelief about the whole situation and felt the system failed me. I fell into a depression and didn't tell anyone about what happened. A couple of months later, I found out I was pregnant. I dropped out of college and later returned to Nashville with a baby. To this day, I've never mentioned him to GG, but I have talked to her often about George, her Godfather."

GG trotted into the kitchen. "Momma, is Godfather George having dinner and watching a movie with us?"

Reba was both shocked and surprised that GG connected the dots.

"Sure, GG, what's for dinner?" George answered for Reba.

"The same thing we have every dinner and movie night, peanut butter and jelly sandwiches. Mommy, I'll get the bread."

Reba told GG not to worry about making a sandwich for her because she wasn't hungry.

Reminding her, GG said, "Momma, you shouldn't be eating after having hot pickles anyways!"

"How did you know I had hot pickles?"

"You forgot to put a stick of gum in your mouth and wipe your hands with a wet wipe before coming to pick me up. When you bent down to hug and kiss me, I had to catch my breath. You reeked of spicy pickles!" GG replied, laughing.

Reba blew her breath into her hands and sniffed. "Does it smell that bad?"

GG and George laughed at Reba.

"Why don't we change the pace and order pizza?" George suggested.

GG exclaimed, jumping up and down with excitement, "I would love to, but only if Momma agrees. Please, momma, please," while flashing her a big smile.

Hesitating, Reba said, "Yes, we can order pizza, my dear."

GG hugged her momma and thanked her.

After watching half of the movie, GG did the usual. She fell asleep. Usually, Reba would pick her up and carry her to her room, but instead, she offered George the opportunity and asked him if he would like to take her and tuck her into bed.

"It would be my honor," he replied.

After watching her sleep for a short moment, he mumbled, "GG, My princess, I will forever be your knight. No one shall ever harm you."

Reba then told George, "Follow me."

He followed her into the bedroom and shut the door behind them.

"I want you to tuck me in, too," she whined.

Reba kissed him and went into the bathroom. George could still hear her talking, "My castle is yours ... Make yourself comfortable."

Trying to loosen up, George sat down on Reba's bed and took off his shoes when he heard a notification alert come from his phone. Contemplating what to do, he saw some paper and a pen on Reba's nightstand and wrote her a note. Inhaling deeply several times, he put his shoes back on before storming out of the house, jumping into his truck, and speeding off.

When Reba came out of the bathroom, she didn't see George. She searched all over for him and realized that he was not in the house. When she looked out the front-room window, she noticed that his truck was gone. She ran to her bedroom and tossed herself onto the bed, thinking to herself, *I wonder if I said or did something wrong again.* Minutes after allowing her emotions to settle down, she pulled back her covers and climbed under them. To her surprise, a bunch of money went flying throughout the bed and onto the floor. She then spotted a note that read:

> *My dearest Reba and GG, I abruptly left because I have an issue that requires my undivided attention. If you're reading this note, you should have seen the money, which is $1500. Please ask GG if there is anything she wants to buy. If so, please get it for her, if it is okay with you, of course. And let her know that I'm missing you guys already and will be returning soon—kisses for you both. I know what you're thinking, but no, I did not vanish on you again. I am coming back. Love, George.*

After arriving home, George went online to order a black maxi dress, black blazer, black shoes, black pantyhose, black clutch, black shades, and a brunette, shoulder-length wig, hoping it would all deliver just in time for the affair.

CHAPTER 27

That Bastard

Devin asked Catrina to stop by and prepare a thank-you note for everyone. To figure out how many cards she needed, she turned to the back of the memory book to see how many people signed it. The last person who signed caused her blood pressure to rise. Stumbling out of her chair, she screamed for Devin. When he entered the room, Catrina had a terrifying look on her face.

"What's up, sis? You okay?"

She said, stuttering, "To- to- toward the back … Lo-, look at the signature toward the back."

Devin picked up the book, flipped to the last page, and read:

Rest in peace, my sweets. George Bojack.

Slamming the book onto the table, he screamed, "THAT BASTARD WAS AT PILAR'S FUNERAL!"

He took off the platinum watch George had given him and threw it at the wall.

"Devin, it's not the watch's fault," Catrina said as she went to retrieve it.

Neither one of them noticed the tiny mechanism that popped out of the watch when it hit the wall, one of the world's smallest GPS.

To be continued…

About The Author

S ofee Sophia, named after the famous actress Sophia Loren, was born in Fort Wayne, Indiana, and is a mother of three biological children and three bonus children. At a young age, Sofee started having visions that evolved into original materials, igniting her passion for film and acting, revealing the evidence of her calling. She has also developed a keen eye for unveiling talent within others. She is a businesswoman, stage and screen playwright, director, actress, and now published author who strives daily to chase her dreams. And because she is an avid believer in Jesus Christ, who is the head of her life, she believes in the manifestation of bringing her dreams to fruition.